THE
SALT MARSH
KING

DREW KREPP

Published by Bancroft Press
"Books that Enlighten"
P.O. Box 65360, Baltimore, MD 21209
410-764-1967 (fax)
www.bancroftpress.com

Cover and Interior Design: J. L. Herchenroeder
Author Photo: Carson Vaughan

ISBN 978-1-61088-149-4 (cloth)
ISBN 978-1-61088-150-0 (mobi)
ISBN 978-1-61088-151-7 (epub)
Printed in the United States

To Jenni, whom I love
and to her father, who loved the water

CONTENTS

CHAPTER ONE	1
CHAPTER TWO	7
CHAPTER THREE	17
CHAPTER FOUR	25
CHAPTER FIVE	45
CHAPTER SIX	53
CHAPTER SEVEN	67
CHAPTER EIGHT	75
CHAPTER NINE	87
CHAPTER TEN	95
CHAPTER ELEVEN	107
CHAPTER TWELVE	127
CHAPTER THIRTEEN	135
CHAPTER FOURTEEN	143
CHAPTER FIFTEEN	153
CHAPTER SIXTEEN	161
CHAPTER SEVENTEEN	177
CHAPTER EIGHTEEN	187
CHAPTER NINETEEN	199
CHAPTER TWENTY	211
ACKNOWLEDGEMENTS	217
ABOUT THE AUTHOR	219

When a child first catches adults out—when it first walks into his grave little head that adults do not have divine intelligence, that their judgments are not always wise, their thinking true, their sentences just—his world falls into panic desolation. The gods are fallen and all safety gone. And there is one sure thing about the fall of gods: they do not fall a little; they crash and shatter or sink deeply into green muck.

—*John Steinbeck,* East of Eden

CHAPTER ONE

The old men still talked about Francesca. They spoke of her in hushed tones the way they spoke of their wives when their wives were in the next room. They talked about her as if she were still somewhere out there, waiting, still not done. They talked about the days afterwards, about the roofs floating out in the sound and the boats washed onto the streets. They talked about the bloated white bodies half-covered with sand, and of the men who got caught offshore and vanished with their boats into the churning void.

Francesca had come like a nightmare; sudden, direct. She came late in the season, one of the big storms that germinate off the coast of Africa and, ever tightening, ever growing, follow the warm currents toward the soft underbelly of southern American coasts.

They saw her coming, but she was supposed to stay offshore.

She was supposed to follow the coast a safe distance out, then come apart in the chilled waters of the North Atlantic.

But she began to shift just north of the South Carolina border. In the dead of night, before the less cautious could escape, she veered violently west and collided with the islands. Her eye passed over Watchman's Island. The surge reached twenty feet and the waters completed what the winds had started. By morning, the island was hewn in two.

The old men still winced when they spoke of that morning. With little provocation, they would tell the terrific battle tale of the storm and the night, of the wind tearing at their roofs and walls that bulged and groaned under the strain and the cropped peaks of waves blown against second-story windows. They spoke of the storm with reverence but with ease. Francesca was the worst, but the big storms formed the timeline of their lives. There had been dozens of them, and the stories were as much a part of them as the storms themselves.

It was the calm that bothered them, not the storm. The calm of the next morning left gaps in their speech where they struggled, unable or unwilling, to find the words. They spoke of the morning only to each other, to those who had also squinted in the unseemly sunshine at the sudden absence of all they had known—to those who did not need the words in the empty spaces of their comrades' speech in order to understand. When the story was trotted out for young people, tourists, and newcomers, it always began with Francesca's landfall and ended abruptly somewhere in the night, as if the speaker had managed to sleep. In the story they told, they never awoke, just trailed off with numbers—wind speeds, the height of the surge—and left it at that.

But the old men told the entire story to Patrick O'Reilly, though he was born after Francesca. They told him because his grandfather had been taken by the storm, and ancestral rights made him a part of their fraternity of shared loss.

It seemed to Patrick that the old men felt they had no right to withhold the tale from him, that they owed it to him because it was, in its way, as much a part of him as it was of them. So when they told the story to Patrick, they paused, grimaced, took a drink or a breath or whatever they needed, and continued, slower, softer, in spite of the empty spaces where the words would not come.

Patrick first heard the story when he was eighteen. With a wink from the owner of the bar, he'd been allowed to sit on one of the barstools and listen to the men talk. That first time was a revelation; his father had spoke neither of the night of the storm nor of the next morning. He had always summed up the storm in a passing phrase—

"Francesca killed your grandfather"—and only when it had to be said. For years, Francesca had existed without description, suspended in some shapeless way in the indefinite past of his family's history, like a disgraced relative of whom no one ever spoke. When the tale unraveled for the first time in its full length, Patrick had been somewhat startled to learn that Francesca had affected other families as well, that not only his grandfather had died, that Francesca was not some assassin who had come in the night for one man.

He had heard the tale dozens of times since. The story varied with the storyteller; each man had seen it a different way. Some spoke of what was there, the wreckage and the saltwater void where part of the island had been, the mocking calm of the water. Some spoke of what was not there at all, of staring at air where houses had stood in the light of the previous day, of the faces missing from the gathered men.

And the roads. They all spoke of the roads, of the two simple flat lengths of asphalt that snaked down the island and had probably never garnered a second thought from anyone until the morning they remained when nothing else was left. Half-covered with sand but still whole, lying amidst piles of collapsed lumber and little square plots of nothing, stretching to a shore that had not been there the night before. They sloped quietly into the water and climbed the new shore on the other side as if directed by some inner will, impervious to wind and indifferent to the distinction between water and land. The roads bothered the men and when they spoke of them they made a gesture, always the same gesture: a flat hand, just above the surface of the bar, moving slowly away, dipping once, then rising and moving away again.

Eventually, Patrick knew each variation by heart. Still the men talked, knowing he had heard, knowing they had told it to him before. So he listened to them tell their stories and was often surprised to hear what words were sometimes missing with each new iteration. He saw the hand move out over the bar and saw the car behind the man's eyes, the phantom car that drove over those roads and, in so doing, put them back together, put it all back the way it had been.

He became fluent in the language of old men speaking and for him, too, the morning after Francesca became harder than the night. He could see the wreckage by the first light of the new calm and feel hope leave, over and over. He could feel the awareness come wordlessly over the bleary-eyed men standing amidst the now-still ruin. He could feel their awful certainty replace the spots where hope had lived in tiny spheres within the swirling darkness. He'd see them shake their gray heads and know that sometimes she still came in the night to rattle the pictures on their walls. He watched them stare at their hands, palms outstretched, and recall younger hands, less arthritic, knuckles less swollen, and fingers less gnarled, still unable to save a neighbor no matter how fast or how hard they worked. And every once in a while, one of them would look at him, directly at him but like he was not there, then quickly away, and Patrick knew that the man was seeing the place where the life they had lived and the life from which he himself had come were joined, knew that this man saw his grandfather that day, saw a dead man then and was seeing him again now.

But Patrick had never met his grandfather. He did not feel the early winds of Francesca against his shoulder in the twilight of that long night and he had never seen Watchman Island whole. He had lived his life entirely within the aftermath and rebuilding. He learned to walk while they finished dredging the channel from the gap between the severed islands back to Spring Tide. He built sandcastles in the island's surf while the men constructed new houses on stilts. He rode a big yellow bus while men laid sod behind the houses on the sound side of the island. And he ran his hands over the first wispy hairs on his chin as he sat mesmerized on the banks of the waterway, watching thick-gloved men waist-deep in the water as they directed the cranes that buried pilings in the mud, building the docks behind the warehouse for the trawlers of Spring Tide.

Then, in the summer of his sixteenth year, his father told him that it was time for him to work, that "O'Reillys work." He knew his father meant for him to work at one of the markets—sweeping floors, offloading boats, cleaning fish—just as his brothers had done. But Patrick had never really taken his eyes off the way the pieces of wood came together in the water, so he went to the house of the man who built docks, whom everyone called Old Man Watts even though he was still in his fifties, and asked him for a job.

And then he set to work.

He learned with his hands and by watching Watts' hands. All he saw and heard and did came slowly together and settled somewhere inside that part of the brain where men who are not afraid to face it keep whatever it is that makes them know who they are. And, in the early days before true awareness had come to him, before his body had matured first by the law of life and later by the work with heavy things, a certainty came to him, a single unfailing constant in a place defined by change: *When the question is* What now? *men build. They do not have to know why. They do not have to build for themselves. It is the building that matters.*

They built Spring Tide even before his father was there. They built on the island, first the lighthouse and the watchman's shack, then the fishermen's houses. Then electricity came and so they built the bridge and, now with heat and light, they added more houses and roads to run between them. Then Francesca came and took away the lighthouse, unbuilt all of the houses south of the watchman's shack, took away lives along with part of the island out from under the houses. The men took a hard look around and they asked the question. Then they built again, and Patrick knew that it was the answer, so he, too, built, always with the imperfect image of Francesca hanging just beyond the horizon.

Sometimes the old men saw him working from their trawlers, a young man building against the storm—strong, careful, deep—with the idea, but without the illusion, of permanence.

CHAPTER TWO

The tap of hard soles on wood caught his attention and broke the steady rhythm of his work. He was used to the soft, rubber scrape of waders and work boots and the deadened pat of bare feet. In time, such sounds melded with the slap of wake against pilings and the laughing screech of gulls and had become a part of the noise that hung perpetually above the water. Rubber soles and bare feet, sea gulls and moving water: all had become a part of his life and his work and were conspicuous only when absent. It was the foreign sound of hard sole shoes that struck a discordant note and caused him to pause.

He did not turn around to identify the owner of the shoes; he already knew the only person who would bother to look for him on the secluded patch of marsh on the sound side of the island. He clenched three nails between his teeth, held a fourth between two fingers, and lined up another plank. He put the nail to the board and hammered it home with a few hard strokes as the footsteps drew closer, then he acknowledged the inevitable with a sigh. He sat back and looked out over the marsh and the sound that lay beyond. This was the part of the job he cherished, and he did not like to be interrupted.

They had labored for weeks in the mud, hauled large things through soft marsh, worked the heavy machinery, driven the pilings, deeply buried the long iron screws, and tied it down with heavy-gauge cable. It had all been done in the hope that this dock would outlive its owner, that when the hurricanes came, they might take the dock to the left or the right, but this one would hold. Yet it was still only a skeleton. It was not a dock until the planks were nailed down.

There was more to be done. There was always more to be done. There were always things that caught the fancy of the homeowners, ways to make the dock unique or useful or more aligned with their tastes and lifestyles: gazebos, built-in bench seats, boat lifts, sun decks. Patrick was indifferent to the additions. He was good at the work and would do it well and oblige any request. But, as far as he was concerned, a dock was complete when the planks were laid. Anything that came after that was nothing more than a series of actions performed until the owner told him to stop.

"I didn't know they made docks this straight," said the owner of the hard-soled shoes as they came to a stop behind him.

"Hey, Jack," said Patrick, speaking around the nails still clenched between his teeth. "How did you know where I was?"

"Come on, Patty. You're not that hard to find."

Patrick turned and looked past Jack Kent at the colossal white structure that stood a gaudy distance from the dock. The house was perched augustly atop a slight hill, shimmering in affluent whiteness in the late afternoon sun and commanding all it surveyed with patrician aloofness. An immaculately manicured lawn swept downward from the house to the marsh over which the dock had been constructed. The wooden dock that jutted out perpendicular to the emerald lawn still seemed a bit too crude and honest amidst such surroundings, but it would have been impractical to build a platinum dock, so wood would have to do.

Jack was starting to look old. His black hair was taking on gray and beating a slow retreat from his forehead. Creases had deepened in the corners of his eyes, a strange touch of weariness on the face of a man who had never seemed tired. But he still stood tall and straight and neither the unyielding stiffness of his posture nor the precise cut of his pristine, dark suit hinted at any weariness about him.

"What have you been doing lately, Patty?"

Patrick squinted into the fading afternoon sun and tried to get a closer look at Jack's face. Jack had always been fond of Patrick, but it was unusual for him to make small talk when he had been sent somewhere by Patrick's father.

"Well, you're standing on it," said Patrick.

Jack turned and appraised once more the long, straight row of planks that trailed behind him.

"So, how is Jessica?" he asked.

"Who?"

"Jessica. Your girlfriend?"

Patrick leaned back over his work. He took a nail from between his teeth and lined it up more carefully than necessary for a plank already secured by two nails. He tapped it a few times until it bit into the wood and stood on its own.

"It's Jennifer. And she's gone," he said, and swung the hammer down hard, driving the nail flush with a single stroke.

"I could have sworn her name was Jessica," said Jack. His voice was inquisitive; he seemed intrigued by his mistake in the way that only those who do not make many can be. "Of course I never met her, but I could have sworn her name was Jessica. I'm certain your father referred to her as Jessica."

"Well, he never met her either. And I'm quite sure her name is Jennifer."

"I see. So, where has she gone?" asked Jack.

"Away from me," said Patrick. "Anyway, what difference does it make?"

Patrick tossed the hammer aside. Something was wrong; Jack was not a man who dallied around the point. Patrick sat back with a grimace and pulled his stiff knees out from under him, rested his feet on the joists not yet planked, and looked hard at Jack.

"Jack, what are you doing here?"

"Your father is having a party this evening at the Delacroix," said Jack without further hesitation, "and he would like you to attend."

Patrick leaned forward and rested his arms on his elbows.

"That's it? A party? He sent you all the way out here to tell me to come to a party?"

"To *ask* you to come to a party."

Patrick sat in silence for a moment. Jack looked out across the sound and waited. Eventually Patrick dismissed with a shrug that which he could not fathom.

"What kind of party? What's it for this time?"

"It is the forty-fifth anniversary of the day he opened his first market."

"Huh. You'd think he'd hold out for fifty. God knows he'll still be at it in five years. Anyway, I don't think I'll be able to make it. I have other plans."

"Patrick, your father would like to see you. He hasn't seen you in a while," said Jack, gently but firmly, and Patrick knew they were Jack's own words and not his father's instructions.

Patrick was not sure what to say. He did not want to argue with Jack. And he did not want to go to a party.

"I suspect that he's going to ask Marie to marry him."

Patrick nodded slowly. He examined the grain of the wood beneath him. "That happened awfully fast," he said, despite his certainty that not saying anything would be best.

Jack's loyalty to Henry O'Reilly extended unquestionably to his sons; Patrick had felt the full force of it on numerous occasions. But he knew there was a fine but firm line between the sons and the man himself, and there was no question on which side Jack stood. He would be the first to question Henry directly and the last to voice doubts to anyone else about Henry's judgment. Patrick's transgression was minor, but he knew he had gone too far.

"The party is at the Delacroix. It begins promptly at nine. I hope to see you there," said Jack. He said it without anger, without hostility, without any emotion at all, but with a finality that silenced any appeal. Then he turned to leave.

"It's good to see you, Jack," said Patrick, by way of an apology, to the back of his suit.

"You too, Patty," he replied, turning around as a faint smile eased its way across his face. "All circumstances aside, your father really would like to see you."

Patrick conceded the point, nodded his acquiescence, and listened to the hard shoes tap once more down the planks. "Careful at the end there," he called as Jack neared the edge of the dock. "It gets a little soggy. Don't want to get those shoes dirty."

Jack gave half a wave without turning around. Patrick heard a faint chuckle as the man stepped carefully over the patch of mud and onto the green lawn.

He sat for a while after Jack had gone. The afternoon light was gathering, waiting, preparing to vanish into night. The first hints of the coming coolness began to tighten around him. It was April and the nights still came early. Soon it would be summer and the warmth of the day would become a paralyzing, crushing heat and sweat would drain from his body in an unceasing stream. In the evenings, the heat would not dissipate and the air would not move. In the afternoons, the summer storms would blow in from the water or creep stealthily up the coast and Patrick would plead with the pregnant clouds: *One more hour. One more half-hour. Ten more minutes. And then you can have the waters to yourself. Five more minutes of work and I'll be gone.*

But it was still spring, still too early for the afternoon storms that would come to fracture his days. Elsewhere in Spring Tide and on the island, in Raleigh and Fayetteville and Ohio and New York and all the places from which the tourists came, the people grew weary of the cold, weary of waiting for the summer, and anxious for weekends at the beach. But Patrick liked April. In the spring, it either rained or it did not. When he woke in the morning, he could tell whether or not he would get in a full day's work; the weather was often erratic, the evenings were not always pleasant, and the days were sometimes too cool for shorts, but if it was going to rain, then it would rain all day. There was no equivocation and he was never blown off a dock by a swift-moving storm, never had to scramble to gather his tools or bargain with a graying sky.

Patrick did the math in his head. A couple more weeks of April, then May. He could get three, maybe four weeks out of May. Maybe even cull something from the first week of June. Then the heavy heat would settle in and the people would come in force. They would fill the island and swarm the streets of Spring Tide. The roads would jam with cars and the waterway with boats. Five weeks at the least, seven at the most. Call it six weeks. Plenty of time.

He stood carefully and stretched the stiffness of the day from his back. He looked at the shadows of the pilings rippling under the running-out tide. *Still early*, he thought. *One more hour, maybe.* Yet he remained staring at the skeleton framework from the end of the dock. He knew he would not go back to work; he would not be able to drown out the thoughts with the pounding of a hammer. He did not want to get in his boat and go home; alone on the water there would be nothing to do but think. He was trapped between an unfinished dock and a solitary ride home.

He had given his men the day off. It would have gone faster with them, but he liked doing this part of the job alone, had come in the early gray of the morning to work among the gently swirling mists. As the hours had passed, the mist burned off and left the day clear and calm, and the daunting pile of planks at the foot of the dock had diminished one by one as he nailed them down, each one another footstep inching closer to the end. Then Jack Kent had come and gone, and now Patrick found himself standing upon a dock three-quarters finished and unable to go on.

He spat onto one of the planks, irritated that some part of him had already decided to go. He picked up his hammer and shoved it under his belt. He gathered his tools, tossed them into his toolbox, and stepped carefully across the naked joists and onto the barge anchored just off the last piling. Then he turned and looked up and down the structure.

He had been at it for seven weeks already. There had been problems from the beginning. Halfway into sinking the pilings, he found that there had once been standing water in that section of the marsh and, during high tide, the middle was too spongy and soft to hold up the massive pilings. They needed to go deeper, to be buried in the firmer mud beneath the soft, upper layer. He had to use longer pilings, and it took an extra week to drive the half-ton behemoths deep enough into the ground to anchor them. Sinking the pilings was always the hardest job, the most time-consuming and dangerous part. Once that was done and the pilings jutted out of the marsh, all went smoothly. The joists were finished in a couple of days, nailed and then cross-bolted onto the pilings. The floating dock was assembled and shackled to the long pilings that stood fifteen feet above water-level at high tide.

And then Mr. Porter became more problematic than soft mud.

"How about if we add another floating dock, Patrick?" he'd asked, a demand framed as a question in the manner of those not often refused.

"How about if we build them perpendicular to the dock?"

"How about we add a boat lift between the floating docks?"

"How about we add benches on the sun deck?"

"I'll be more than happy to pay for the additional work," he always added, as if there was ever any uncertainty about who was going to pick up the tab. But Patrick always acquiesced, revising estimates as needed and smiling inwardly every time Mr. Porter said the word "we." "We," he thought to himself each time. *As if he is out here helping us build the damn thing.*

Yet it did not matter. He got paid to work, and the more he worked, the more he got paid. But as the Porter job dragged on, he began to worry. He still had to build Mr. Macready's dock, and he had promised he'd have it done by the time Mr. Macready's grandchildren were out of school for the summer.

Mr. Macready lived on the waterway a few miles north of Patrick's house. He had lost his dock to a hurricane a few years prior, shortly after he had retired and moved permanently to Spring Tide. He hadn't bothered to have it replaced. He knew the storms; he knew the risk. He kept his precious fishing boat at the marina and drove the few miles there whenever he wanted to take it out.

But his grandchildren were growing up. They were old enough now to appreciate the water, old enough for him to teach them how to fish. In the summer, his children brought them on the weekends, but the eldest two were old enough to stay for as long as a week or two by themselves. Mr. Macready no longer wanted to waste time driving. He wanted the boat waiting for him in his backyard.

He wanted his dock rebuilt.

"Just need some place to keep my boat. It don't have to be nothing fancy," he'd said.

Patrick liked him immediately.

So Patrick agreed to build it and promised to finish it by the summer. It was a straightforward job. A straight dock with a boat-lift at the end. Simple. The dock would be short. The work would go fast.

Patrick had already discovered the Porters' soft mud when Mr. Macready made his request, but he still had plenty of time. Then Mr. Porter began his series of congenial demands. So Patrick worked long and hard to satisfy Mr. Porter's whims, all the while feeling for the weather with the back of his neck.

And then it had come, just a few days before. The first hot day, the first day of the year when he could feel the true heat, the hot uncomfortable Southern heat with its tangible weight and depth and thickness that heat shouldn't have and temperatures can't convey. It would oscillate, of course; the nights would still be cool and so would some of the days for a while yet. But with that first hot day, Patrick knew the pendulum had swung and that summer, inexorably, was on its way.

He stood on the barge, vexed by the incomplete planking, and did the math once more. It came out the same. Six weeks. Maybe seven. Two more weeks at the Porters, then Mr. Macready. He could still get it done; there was still time.

He dropped the toolbox into the bow of the johnboat he kept tied fast to the barge. He untied the bowline, flung it over the toolbox, and climbed into the boat. The motor sputtered to a low growl, emitted a dull gray belch of smoke. He untied the stern line and kicked off the barge.

Plenty of time.

CHAPTER THREE

The boat swung out into the sound in a long, slow arc that brought him alongside the marshlands between the sound and the waterway. On most days, the ride home gave him time to be still, to measure the work done against the work yet to be done, to release himself from the daily race against the path of the sun and indulge in the fatigued satisfaction of exhaustion before the soreness settled into his shoulders. But most days didn't end with Jack Kent coming to find him.

He lowered the throttle and let the current carry him as he approached the inlet. The tide was low, too low, and he knew it but looked wistfully toward the inlet anyway. There were two paths through the marsh to his house. The channel, wide and accessible, was half a mile south of the Porter house. The inlet, shallow and hazardous, untended by man, was directly across the sound from the Porter house and opened onto the waterway only a few hundred feet from his dock. It only shaved five or ten minutes off the trip to use the inlet, and the detour via the channel seldom bothered him but, at the moment, he was trying to avoid thinking, so a quiet boat ride along those reflective waters was less than ideal.

He peered at the narrow, white smoothness of the still-wet sandbar that stretched across the inlet's mouth. He opened the throttle back up.

It's only a party. They're all the same. An hour, maybe two.

He forced the thought out of his head and looked to see if he could spot the roof of his house, even though he knew where it was and that it would not come into view until he passed the flat island of huddled trees squatting among the marsh reeds.

The tide was not right. That was the problem. The inlet simply was not navigable at low tide. The sandbar across the mouth was only one of many. They stood out of the water at every turn, shining white by day and glowing ghostly in the night, forever growing and shifting and vanishing as the waters incessantly built and shaped and destroyed them. Closer to the banks, the oyster beds arched jagged from the calm like the scaled tail of some great beast. But the obstructions were visible at low tide and so there was no excuse for being hampered by them. Patrick had seen it happen on more than a few occasions, seen either arrogance or ignorance run a boat aground on one of the inlet's menaces and leave it beached, hull exposed, listing at an odd angle one way or the other, bulging and bloated and clumsy.

There was no excuse for trying the inlet at low tide.

At high tide, however, the sandbars and oyster beds were at their most treacherous. The waxing waters slip silently over their surfaces, covering them until the reflection of the water belies their existence, covering them like night covers sin.

Patrick had seen dozens of boats fall prey to the subversions of the inlet at high tide, to the inviting lie of calm water. Even an experienced waterman could be deceived. And the inlet at high tide was less forgiving. Beached at low tide was a waiting game; the waters always came back. More often than not the tide runs out from under a boat run aground at high tide and the uneven weight can crack the hull and the boat becomes nothing at all. Or worse than nothing. Flotsam.

Patrick knew the inlet and always took the risk if the tide was right. He knew the oyster beds by memory; he could see them in his mind as if the water wasn't there. The sandbars were forever in motion and could not be memorized but he knew the signs, the jetties and the bends where the current could be broken and the sand shaken free from it to collect on the bottom. And he could spot the flat sections of water, the long, narrow ovals of calm amidst the ripples that told him the bottom was only an inch or two away.

Even as he motored away from the mouth of the inlet, he considered it. He measured the flat-hulled boat's displacement against the progress of the tide and weighed his odds. Ultimately, however, that which he knew, he knew too well, and would not take the risk. He twisted the throttle to its maximum and made for the channel in earnest.

You know you're going to go. You know you're going to go and you're just trying to find a reason to make it OK.

He shoved it away once more and stared out at the trees that floated past on his right. The trees were bent low and gnarled, massed together in clumps amidst the waist-high reeds and patches of mud worn smooth by the changing tides. The trees all leaned toward the mainland and appeared to Patrick as if they had been caught in motion, frozen in some shared, futile attempt to escape the constant salt winds that blew across the sound and berated them from the east.

The line came into view, the seam in the water where the flat, easy sound met the thick chop of the channel. It was too easy. There was nothing to distract him, no sandbars or reefs, no shallows or bends. The channel was broad and deep, carefully marked and constantly dredged to keep it cleared for the trawlers and cruisers that brought in fish from the ocean and money to Spring Tide.

The bow bounced along as it fought the current. A fine spray flung backwards and stung his eyes. He did not want to slow down so he angled the boat toward the far bank of the channel to cut down on the spray.

What is it in your head that makes you think going faster will make it go away?

He fought it away one more time but knew he had lost. He could see the point in the distance, the jagged edge of mud that marked the juncture of the channel and the waterway. Just off the point, an osprey stabbed downward, tumbled from the sky as if by error, then slapped hard against the surface. It flailed for an instant, its wings churning hard against the water, suddenly graceful, rose dripping and vanished into the trees with a shining silver prize clutched in its talons.

Patrick stared at the flat surface where the strike had been made. The rippling outward from the center mesmerized him for just long enough, and he was back on the Porters' dock for a moment, staring at the creases in the corners of Jack Kent's eyes.

"The Delacroix."

He repeated it. He did not understand why his father made them go all the way to Raleigh. There were a few who lived there, but most of the invitees were from points along the coast.

As a child, the parties had thrilled him. Drinking ginger ale from fancy glasses, hiding under tables with the other children, weaving his way through a sea of well-dressed legs, staying up past his bedtime— it was all thrilling and new, always new. Later, amidst a blossoming awareness of his father's stature, he had found pride and a tantalizing sense of significance at the parties. He thought there was truth in the kindness and respect the guests showed him. When he became aware that they spoke of him when he was not there, the veil fell and it became clear to him why they were so nice.

It had nothing to do with him at all. They were nice to Henry O'Reilly's son because he was Henry O'Reilly's son. They wanted to know what Henry's boy was doing, to know what he would become. And, once they knew, they could measure his intentions and his worth, they could gauge his risk and his value to them.

He had fought it for a while, even long after he had grown aware that he no longer felt how he was supposed to feel about the guests and the crystal and the air inside the Delacroix. He thought something was missing from him that should have been innate, some sense of superiority and worth, of entitlement not earned but nonetheless deserved. And he was at first ashamed at what was missing, ashamed in the way that a child born different than the others learns shame first and all else later.

He fought by showing up, by doggedly continuing to show up at the parties under the misguided belief that he could somehow explain himself and that they would listen. He kept going to the parties long after he had gotten into much-discussed trouble in his teenage years, long after the rumors had swirled around his leaving school, even after the shame left him and was replaced by an ever-strengthening conviction that the whole thing, the parties and the people and everything they said and did, was ugly and distorted and, above all else, small.

When nothing changed, pragmatism broke him away from them.

He had to work on Fridays. It was that simple. The parties were invariably held on Thursday evenings; the weekends were busy at the markets and restaurants, and his father insisted that the managers be able to attend. So he held the parties on Thursdays. Patrick had projects to finish and deadlines that didn't allow for long weekends. So he simply stopped going; it was easier that way. And he found that he felt better not going to the parties where his attendance had proved over and over again to be worthless.

Four years.

He had never put the time together before, not in any linear sense, but as the boat rounded the point and beat against the chop of the waterway, time stretched itself out and made itself known. He had not been in four years.

Four years since he had felt a roomful of eyes on him, since he had been in the same room with his father and his brothers and their wives on any day other than Thanksgiving. He still received the invitations, but he did not think about them when they arrived. He didn't even open them anymore. He didn't feel the slightest compulsion to read the carefully-etched lettering on the heavy gilded paper. They came in the mail and he threw them away, and hadn't realized, until that moment, that he had been doing it for four unbroken years.

His dock came into view around a bend and he knew that he would go. He would go because he had to see for himself. There was a reason Jack had come to him and he had to know. He had to see his father.

He cut the engine just past the dock and let the current push him back against it. He looped the lines neatly around the cleats and made the boat fast and tried to ignore the anxiety his decision had left with him. Halfway down the dock, he heard barking and saw the dark shape moving frantically back and forth behind the blur of the screened-in porch.

"Easy, Neptune. Easy," he called out, trying to make his bellowing voice sound soothing.

He had already had to fix two German Shepherd-sized holes in the porch screens where Neptune had been unable to restrain his jubilation. Neptune always celebrated Patrick's arrival, his enthusiasm never diminished by the daily repetition of the ritual.

Patrick had named the dog "Neptune" because, as a puppy, he was, at least in Patrick's estimation, the single living creature least like the vengeful, bellicose god. He thought it would be funny, but most people didn't get it; most assumed the dog was so named as some sort of kitschy beach ideal or to form a matching set with Poseidon the cat who had come with the house. Neptune had grown up, and his fierce bark and black-shrouded eyes now lent a hint of malevolence to him, but it wasn't there. He remained as harmless and un-godlike as he had been as a pup.

The screen door clacked shut behind Patrick and Neptune leapt at him, half-barking and half-whining, before sprinting out the door. He performed a triumphant victory lap around the yard and hurtled back inside. Patrick knelt beside him, rubbed his head behind the ears, and tried to keep the tongue away from his face.

"Who knows, Neptune? Maybe this thing with Marie isn't all bad," he said, the dog looking at him eagerly but without comprehension as he awaited a word that he understood. "And it'll be good to see Suzanne and the kids."

Poseidon, unimpressed, rolled languidly on his side and looked down upon the scene from his perch atop a crossbeam. Patrick stood and rubbed the cat under the chin. Poseidon extended a paw, unsheathed its claws, and buried them leisurely into the screen.

The dog followed Patrick inside the house, loping along with a self-important gait, his tail at full salute. Patrick filled the bowl in the kitchen and the dog forgot about him. Left on his own once more, Patrick slumped onto the couch, leaned his head back, and closed his eyes. Fatigue rolled over him. Most evenings he barely made it off the couch. Feeding the dog was usually his last obligation. With the day put neatly away, all that remained was a decision between similarly-colored boxes in the freezer and finding something on television that was unobtrusive enough to fall asleep to undisturbed.

"Reow," said the cat as it sauntered into the house.

"Aw, Poseidon," Patrick replied without opening his eyes. "You only find me when I'm comfortable."

The cat leaped onto the couch and pressed its head against Patrick's shoulder.

"It's been a long day, Poseidon."

The cat pressed its paw against his shirt and began to knead.

"And I can't take tomorrow off. I'd have to come back tonight."

"Reow," said the cat again.

He opened his eyes and stroked the cat's head. It purred but did not stop kneading his shirt.

"You don't care, do you? You probably knew I was going the whole time, didn't you?"

The cat rolled onto its side and pressed all four paws into Patrick's legs.

"If my boat sounded like you, I'd have one less problem," he said as he pulled off his boots and threw them onto the floor. He leaned back and closed his eyes once more. He began to slip away, but the thought brought him back: *It'll be good to see the kids.*

"Fine. I'll go. You happy now, Poseidon?"

He heaved himself to his feet with a groan. The cat did not seem to notice.

CHAPTER FOUR

The tuxedo no longer fit quite right. It was long enough but too tight in the shoulders and every time he raised his arms the sleeves pulled up too far. The thin cloth of his suit pants had the unpleasant feel of lost familiarity. The bow tie pinched his throat more than he remembered, and the cummerbund, which had never fit well, now sagged even more loosely around his waist than it had the last time he had worn it.

He had never worn suits well; he had never quite learned how to move in them. They always made him feel like he was wearing someone else's clothes and he could never fully get his mind off an imperfectly-tied bow tie or the shirt that kept coming untucked on one side.

The lobby of the Delacroix had the clean smell of nothing. Not the sterile-clean smell of a hospital but the carefully maintained complete absence of smell that was as much a product of meticulous design as the leather couches and mahogany-paneled walls, the paintings of muted nudes and the lighting dimmed to a precise brightness enabling one to recognize another yet not obligate them to make any point about having done so.

Past the elevators and down a hallway marked "Private," Patrick came to a stop in front of a young man commandeering a podium situated in front of two doors above which was mounted a brass plaque reading, "The O'Reilly Room." The man was dressed identically to Patrick but appeared far more comfortable in his attire despite his generally round-shouldered posture.

"Good evening, Mr. O'Reilly," he said.

Patrick muttered a greeting in response, some mild, polite protest at being addressed as "Mr. O'Reilly." The young man swung open the doors and, for a moment, Patrick could see only specks of light in the dim room, shimmering from the chandeliers above and glistening on the crystal glasses and on the bottles behind the bar. He could hear glasses clinking, the soft chirp of women laughing, and the muted buzz of conversation beneath the delicate sound of a string orchestra.

He eased into the room and stood still until the doors closed behind him. His eyes adjusted to the meager light and the party resolved itself from its shadows. He saw before him a sea of people, women enshrouded in gowns set off by men in black suits and ties, some moving, some seated, some cloistered in stern conversation, some gathered in humorous levity. The faces came last, numerous and half-familiar, many inspecting him with varying degrees of subtlety. He did not see his father or either of his brothers and so, reluctant to jump cold into the heart of the thing, he edged his way over to the bar.

The bartender was an older man whose face detailed a life behind the bar. He appeared to be afloat, moving steadily and without haste. He seemed to be somehow apart from the glittering shapes that swirled around him, distant from them in some way, as if he had been at it for so long that his body worked from memory, leaving the rest of him free to go wherever it pleased.

"Whiskey," Patrick said. Calculating the time and the place, he added, "And water. Whiskey and water." Then he added, "Please."

He took a cautious sip, then a less cautious one.

He loathed uncertainty. It made him uncomfortable and being uncomfortable made him feel like being alone. And when he could not be left alone, the uncertainty became a jumbled sort of frustration and desperation that made him feel as though he was drowning.

He turned toward the party, taking care not to look too long at anyone or to make eye contact lest he be forced to recall names and conjure something of pleasant inconsequence to say. It seemed strange to him that no one had yet approached him, but he figured it had been some time and no one knew him well enough to know what to say. But he didn't really mind standing at the bar by himself. What bothered him was that he could feel himself bracing for something and was not sure what it was.

He was waiting; he knew he was waiting, that he had to be waiting for something or else he wouldn't still be there. He also knew that Jack would come to find him, to be polite and to feel him out before Henry made his presence known.

Finally, Patrick spotted Jack moving through the crowd toward the bar, neither smiling nor shaking hands as he moved and not looking at Patrick either, though he was, without question, heading for him.

"Another water and tonic, Jack?" Patrick asked before the bartender had a chance.

Jack smiled at the reference. At any social function, Jack ordered one vodka tonic at the beginning of the evening and then had the bartender fill the same glass with water on ice for the rest of the night. It was less an attempt at subterfuge than at lightness. It was an accouterment, the sum total of his effort to be a participant in a social gathering rather than a boss.

"How are you this evening, Patty? You having a good time?"

"Sure. Where is he?"

"He's around. He'll be out in a moment, I'm sure."

The two men fell quiet, slowly drinking their drinks, real and imaginary, and staring with neither interest nor motive at the undulating mass of expensive clothing. A thought came to Patrick and he broke the silence first, more out of boredom than anything that might have emanated naturally from the silence.

"Hey, who's the guy at the door?"

Jack looked probingly at Patrick.

"You don't recognize him?"

"You have any idea how few people I know?"

"That's Doug Castin."

"*Dougie* Castin? You're kidding me."

"Be a pretty bad joke if I were."

"I didn't recognize him," he said. "I didn't even say anything to him. He must be, what? Twenty years old by now?"

"Twenty-two, Patty. He's graduated from college and works for your father."

"He's always worked for my father. What's his job now?"

"He is your father's assistant."

"Everyone's my father's assistant," replied Patrick. "What exactly does he assist with?"

"Presently, he's assisting your father by keeping track of the guests at this party," Jack said, and in the tone of his voice, Patrick heard the finality, the thin unbreakable metal that meant the polite but indisputable end of a conversation.

"I guess it beats mowing lawns," said Patrick. "I should have said something to him."

In a passable effort at casualness, Jack brushed away any potential offense with a flick of his wrist. "I doubt he thought anything of it."

Without further preamble, Jack moved away from the bar and was gone. Patrick knew where he had gone. He ordered another drink and waited.

Patrick felt it before he heard it, the palpable stiffening, the shift of an entire room's demeanor, as if the guests had lost themselves in the wine and liquor and dimmed lights and then, in the space of a moment, remembered collectively where they were and why. The noises changed, the uniform flutter of conversation slipped into a subdued, unified calm gathered around the center of an intense bustling noise.

His father finally hove into view, shaking hands and splashing his drink indiscriminately among the cluster of people orbiting him. He was flanked on his right by Marie Bouchard. Patrick had met her only once and she had worn the same fixed smile that was radiant but without warmth. Her hair was swept into a blondish-gray crown and she kept herself pinned to Henry's side. Patrick's brothers stayed close to the same nucleus, Sean vigilantly maintaining his position on his father's left and Bryan shuffling along behind. Sean nodded magnanimously and with self-importance at the people his father addressed; Bryan hardly spoke at all, his head cast at its usual downward angle.

"Patty, my boy!" The sound boomed like cannon fire above the crowd and all heads turned. Patrick's jaw tightened. His father moved toward him with the space-clearing carriage of one who is constantly surrounded by people. The crowd churned around him as he came. Then it was in front of Patrick, all around him. His father extended a large hand and Patrick shook it. He could feel the roughness of the hand, the only part of Henry O'Reilly that had not softened after the years had separated him from the hard work of his youth. Sean and Bryan shook hands with Patrick as well while Marie held hers daintily aloft. Patrick shook it, unsure whether or not she intended for him to kiss it.

"You remember Marie, of course?" said his father.

"It's a pleasure to see you again, Patrick," said Marie.

"You too."

They stood awkwardly, Patrick with his back to the bar facing a semicircle of faces that smiled expectantly at him, his father beaming red-faced among them. He looked around for an escape path; it was a habit he had developed in circumstances involving crowds and he had done it for as long as he could remember. In his periphery, Patrick could see people bend their heads to others' ears as they watched.

Seconds passed and Patrick wondered if they expected an impromptu speech from him. Instinctively, he looked to Jack for some sort of cue, but Jack looked back at him with the faintest hint of a grimace and shrugged. At last, his father put an arm around him.

"Patty, let's introduce you around. You might remember some of these folks. How long's it been since you've come to one of these?"

But he was not listening for a response. Henry guided him through the party and made introductions and explanations as they went. Patrick shook hands and nodded, disregarding names and answering "yes" without thinking every time he was asked whether or not he remembered this person or that. They whirled their way through investors, restaurateurs, and friends of the O'Reillys until Patrick found himself finally facing someone he knew well.

"You remember Charles Porter, of course?" said Henry.

Porter stood frozen, looking from father to son. A snort of laughter escaped Patrick. He knew that Mr. Porter was caught in an impossible social quandary, trapped between a man of great influence, whose respect was a prized commodity, and the man's son, who worked in the mud behind his house.

"Sure. I'm building his dock."

Patrick did not look at his father but could feel him stiffen at his side. He knew that the joviality had vanished, as it always did, and that his father found nothing amusing about the encounter.

Mr. Porter, however, had regained his composure and seemed determined to blast his way through the awkwardness with an effusion of words. "And quite a nice job he's doing, I might add. Very . . . nice. Very nice job. Everything looks great. Couldn't be happier. Quite a skilled craftsman, your son. Been meaning to tell you that."

Patrick thanked Mr. Porter and suppressed a smile as best he could. Henry, however, muttered an excuse, gripped Patrick around his upper arm, and attempted to pull him away. His father was a large man and still carried his years as a fisherman around his shoulders, but the years had caught up with him and Patrick was far too strong to be moved without consent.

"You're not going to drag me out of here. I don't give a damn what your problem is."

"You will come with me right now," said Henry, almost hissing as he spoke through his teeth, fighting to keep his voice down. Patrick did not move.

"Don't you dare cause a scene here, Patty."

"I'm not causing a scene. I'm speaking in a low tone and I haven't done anything wrong."

Before Patrick was fully aware that he was nearby, Jack slid between him and his father. He put a hand on Henry's wrist and eased the grip from Patrick's arm.

"Let's take this somewhere more private," he said quietly in Patrick's ear. Then to Mr. Porter, "If you'll excuse us, Charles."

Mr. Porter, wide-eyed, looked from Henry to Jack.

"Of course," said Mr. Porter. "Certainly. No problem."

Patrick looked at Jack. He could almost feel the night air, the cool, open breeze that was so close if only he could just take a few steps toward the door. He could almost taste his escape. Instead, he followed Jack and Henry to a small meeting room adjoining the ballroom and Jack closed the door behind them.

"What the hell was that all about?" his father demanded.

"What are you talking about?"

"Do you have any idea who Charles Porter is?"

"Yes, I do. He's my client."

"Look here, Patrick. I didn't work this hard to have a son who's some kind of construction worker. I've had enough of all this nonsense. You're what, thirty-one? Thirty-two?"

"I'm twenty-nine, Dad."

"Well, you're old enough to stop all this foolishness. It's time you took some responsibility."

Patrick looked hard at his father, trying to find some understanding, or at least some semblance of a misunderstanding.

He saw only the large, red face staring back at him.

"We've been talking about this forever. I'm done now," said Patrick.

Henry rolled his eyes upward and exhaled heavily from his nose.

"I have tried with you, Patty. I really have. I've been as patient as I could be," he said. "But you just will not listen to reason."

"Jesus, Dad. I'm good at what I do. I have people that depend on me. I'm not just being stubborn."

Henry jabbed a finger in Patrick's direction. "That is no kind of life for you, out there in the mud. There's no future in it. It's an embarrassment."

"We're not talking about this again. I'm not letting you bait me into this discussion again."

"There won't be any more discussion. You're right about that. You will go back and finish with college. And then you will come to work for this company the way the rest of your family does. And that's my final word."

Patrick stepped closer to his father. He heard Jack move closer behind him. Patrick leaned in until he was no more than a foot away from Henry's face and spoke slowly.

"Your 'final word' hasn't meant a damn thing to me in years."

Henry laughed, derision curling his mouth.

"Think you don't need the old man anymore? Well, you like that house you've been living in rent-free? We'll see how you feel when I sell it out from under you."

"Have you lost your mind? That house is mine. Mom made sure of that. You remember my mother, right? Gave birth to your children?"

In a sudden practiced motion, Henry's arm lashed out and the back of his hand struck Patrick hard across the face. Patrick's jaw clenched and his arm drew back as the sting bit at him. A decision flashed through his mind; ragged incomplete bits of information failed to sort themselves as he stood with his arm half-drawn and fury roiling inside him. But he did not swing. He did not know why.

Jack moved closer and stood between them with his back to Patrick. He kept his arms by his side and stared at Henry until Henry looked back at him.

The old man was breathing heavily and his face quivered with rage. Then he took a step back.

Patrick unclenched his fist.

"You already tried to take my house, remember?" said Patrick, speaking without emotion, almost without sound. "A few years ago. After a conversation a lot like this one. I had your lawyers at my door for six months. But Mom made sure that house was in my name before she died and there's nothing you or any of your people can do about it. And I don't live there rent-free. I pay the mortgage. It's mine."

Henry glowered at Patrick, his lips twitching, trying to shape words. He stood swollen with rage a moment longer, then brushed past Patrick and slammed the door on his way out.

When he was gone, Patrick sat in a chair at the table and stared at the corner of the room. Jack took a seat opposite him but did not look at him.

"What the hell, Jack?" said Patrick.

"Please trust me when I tell you that this is not why your father wanted you to be here tonight."

"Well, what did he expect? That I'd come here and he'd say for the thousandth time, 'Hey Patty, go back to school, then come work for me,' and this time it would be different? I swear to God, Jack, I don't know where he got the idea that he's the only man alive who gets to have everything he wants."

"Patrick, as hard as it may be to believe, it wasn't always this way for him."

"I know, I know. He worked his way up from nothing and all of that."

"Yes, he did. Think about where he came from. He was the son of an immigrant laborer. He started working on a fishing boat when he was fifteen because he had no other choice. He lost two brothers to the ocean and a third to a war, and their loss probably cost him his mother as well. And now he owns the biggest fishing and seafood wholesaler in the Southeast. An entire town owes their livelihood to him. Believe me, Patrick, I remember the down times. I remember all the families leaving Spring Tide. I remember my father having to drive into Wilmington to look for work. But your father refused to leave. He saved that town, and I know for a fact that it would have been much easier for him to have just left."

"That's great for him, Jack. But what—"

"I'll tell you what it has to do with you. Your father worked since he was a kid just to have a chance at having a chance. Now he's got everything and the last thing in the world he wants is to see his son squandering the chance to have things a little easier than he had."

"I like what I do. And I'm good at it. If that wasn't part of his big plan, then maybe he shouldn't have told me to get a job when I was sixteen."

"He just wanted you to appreciate the value of a hard day's work, that's all. He wants you to pick up where he left off, not retrace his steps," Jack said.

"Well, that's not his call to make. Look at Bryan. He seem like a happy guy to you? He's a forty-year-old man who hasn't made a single decision on his own in fifteen years. I won't do it."

Jack held his hands up, his palms facing Patrick.

"Patty, I'm not telling you that you should. As far as I'm concerned, you have every right to do as you please, and I think you've done just fine for yourself. My point is that there's more to your father's wishes than the desire to have his own way."

Patrick leaned back in his chair and rubbed his eyes.

"Jack, is there any chance that my father forgot about trying to take my house?"

"I wouldn't think so. Why do you ask?"

"I don't know. No reason."

Patrick stood to leave and Jack rose with him.

"Well, as much fun as this has been, I'd better head home," said

THE SALT MARSH KING

Patrick.

"Given the circumstances, I completely understand. But you're sure I can't persuade you to stay for your father's announcement?"

"With all due respect to you, I don't really give a damn what he has to say. There is no way in hell I'm staying here."

Jack held out his hand and smiled. "Fair enough."

Inside the ballroom, there had been no change in demeanor. The party hung in perpetuity within the light-speckled darkness.

Patrick was no more than three steps away from the meeting room door when he felt someone grab him by the elbow. He turned to face the scowling countenance of Sean.

"Let go of my arm."

"I don't know what you said to Dad, but you need to learn a little tact. This is neither the time nor the place to be airing whatever little problem you've got with him."

"Let go of my arm. Right now."

"You need to lay off of Dad. He can't have someone getting him riled up. Not at an event like this. Do you understand me?"

Patrick spoke in a whisper. "This is your last chance to let go of my arm. Do *you* understand *me*?"

Patrick's stare was unwavering. He saw fear flicker across Sean's face but did not need to have seen it to know it was there. Sean released his grip.

"When are you going to learn, Patty? You can't just bully everyone into doing what you want. Out here in the real world, no one's impressed with how strong you are."

"I don't bully anyone. You're thinking of your boss."

"Nothing changes, does it, Patty?" Sean was speaking loudly now, his voice trending upward as it edged toward a falsetto. "Just a spoiled brat who does as he pleases. You need to grow up, kid."

Several of the party guests had heard them and were exchanging significant glances with each other, tantalized at the prospect of a public spat. Patrick noticed the audience and turned to leave.

"Oh, that's right. Run away. Run away like you always do," Sean called at Patrick's back.

Patrick moved steadily toward the door with his head down, focused on his escape. He was within arm's reach when he saw Bryan angling toward him through the crowd.

"Bryan, I don't want to be rude, but the last place on this earth you want to be right now is between me and that door."

"Still working construction, huh, Patty?"

"What?"

"I said 'still working construction.' Back home?"

Bryan was standing with his hands in his pockets, gazing alternately at Patrick's shoes, his own shoes, and an indeterminate spot somewhere behind Patrick. Plunging headlong into middle age, he had the appearance of a former athlete gone badly to seed. The lean muscle had lost its tone and the stomach had expanded; his tall, strong build had lapsed into a stooped, balding, rounded physique. And at some point during his decline, he had lost any sense of pride. He stood before Patrick looking both apathetic and disheveled though he was neither.

"Bryan, I was just leaving."

"So, tell me this: You ever thought about expanding? You know, working more as a contractor? Set up different crews and supervise them instead of doing all the work yourself?"

"What the hell are you talking about?"

"I was just thinking. You can't make any money doing what you're doing. You've got to get other people to start making money for you. That's the only way. No way to make money in construction unless you're at the top."

"Look, I build docks. I don't want to open dock-building franchises."

He did not want to be angry at Bryan. Nor did he want to discuss his business with him. He wanted to shake Bryan, to grab him by the shoulders and shake him until whatever was left of him snapped to attention so that he would no longer have to pity him. But he couldn't, so he did the next best thing. He walked past him without another word and pushed through the door.

He passed Doug Castin again on the way out but was in no mood to rectify his prior inadvertent snub. He turned a corner, found a deserted corridor, and sat down on a bench. He breathed slowly, deliberately, consciously. He rubbed the bridge of his nose. He was not sure why he was sitting there. He was not sure why he had come. He was not sure why he had not yet left.

He heard a commotion around the corner, a woman's stern, scolding voice and angry, snapping footsteps. The woman cleared the corner, half-dragging a small child by the hand as he struggled to keep up. Neither she nor the child saw Patrick as she stopped, spun, and leaned over him.

"This is why we can't take you to places like this. Because you don't know how to behave."

Patrick recognized Bryan's wife Helen, slim, dark-haired, and hard-faced. She was not raising her voice but there was no tenderness in it and no hint of compassion. The child looked up at her, his eyes mournful but fighting tears.

"But Mommy—" said the child, voice quavering.

"But nothing! There are important people here and you've done nothing but embarrass me. Look at yourself!"

Patrick saw a red stain on the child's shirt, the source of her rage.

"But Mommy, I was—"

The hand came down sharply on the small face. The boy's body jerked. He stood motionless, mouth open, stunned. Patrick winced. He felt the muscles tense between his shoulder blades and up the back of his neck. The child spotted Patrick and began to sob. His mother stiffened and looked over her shoulder. She straightened upright.

"You know he's only crying because he saw you."

"Christ, Helen. He's probably crying because you hit him."

She rolled her eyes. Patrick knew she held no regard for him. She worked within a system of money and stature, of hierarchy and proximity, and Patrick was a supernumerary floating around that system having been tethered to it by birth. As such, he was to be tolerated and nothing more. She had married a man whom she knew to be weak and had pushed him to claw his way to his father's side, to take his rightful place alongside Sean. Yet Patrick had shown nothing but disregard for his familial claim. To Helen, it was unforgivable, and Patrick knew his very existence stood as a mockery to all she valued.

It had never occurred to her that the O'Reillys were not royalty.

She stood with her hands on her hips and her jaw thrust in the air, staring her disdain at Patrick. Patrick ignored her, knelt by the child.

"Hi, Henry. Do you remember me?"

The boy sniffled, nodded. He had stopped crying everywhere but his eyes. Patrick ruffled his hair.

"What's my name?"

"Unca Pat."

"That's right. Can Uncle Pat have a hug?"

The boy inched closer and leaned against Patrick. He caught him under the armpits and hoisted him into the air. The child laughed. Helen had had enough.

"Come along, Henry. Let's see if you can behave yourself. I didn't bring a change of clothes for you, so you can just wear that. Maybe that will teach you a lesson."

"He's three years old, Helen."

"That has nothing to do with it!" she said, wagging a finger. "Now put my son down. Some of us have obligations to tend to. *Some* of us have family that we spend time with."

"It's not your family," said Patrick.

He was not at all threatened by Helen. In fact, he found her mildly comical most of the time. But he wanted to make her angry and he knew how to do it.

She stood quivering, her lips pressed hard together. But she had been at it too long to make such a mistake. She turned and, towing the child behind her, strode back down the hallway.

Patrick watched them go. He knew that his nephew's only chance to be worth a damn was to find a strength far beyond anything the boy's father had ever found and a compassion that his mother was incapable of teaching him. He hurt for the child.

Having at last had enough, Patrick headed back down the hall and was passing through the lobby when he heard a woman call his name.

"You've got to be kidding me," he said under his breath but, as he turned, he lost all trepidation. Suzanne, Sean's big-hearted wife, was bearing down on him, her two sons barely keeping pace and her daughter trailing well behind. The little girl, small even for a two-year-old, wore a fluffy white dress and, as she struggled to keep up with her brothers, she looked like a bit of tissue paper blowing across a floor.

Suzanne caught up with Patrick and pulled him into a hug so enthusiastic that Patrick, caught off guard, nearly lost his footing. She bore a rosy-cheeked, slightly harried countenance that seemed always to be smiling whether or not she was. She was a mother, in all senses and at all times; so much so, in fact, that if Patrick stood too close to her for too long, she tried to mother him. She was so completely given to the task that Patrick often wondered what it was she had done with herself before she had kids.

"Patrick! It's so wonderful to see you! Boys, don't be shy. Give your uncle a hug. Clarissa, sweetheart, remember your Uncle Pat? This is your Uncle Pat. Sean mentioned that you might be coming, but I was afraid I'd missed you!"

Patrick hugged the boys; the older boy, pushing the limits of hugging age, reluctantly complied with his mother's wishes. The little girl clung to the back of her mother's leg.

"I was actually on my way out," said Patrick.

"This is my granddad's party," Mickey, the younger of the boys, informed Patrick.

"It sure is, buddy. They all are."

"So, Patrick, how have you been? We never see you anymore," said Suzanne. "Have you been keeping busy?"

"Yeah, I suppose so. Pretty much the same as always."

"Well, you look fit and trim. The work must suit you."

"It's my granddad's party," announced Mickey once more. "He's here for his renouncement."

"Announcement, Mickey. *UH*-nouncement," said Sean Junior, embarrassed by his brother's malapropism. "Gaw," he added, to underscore his disgust.

"That's right, sweetie. Granddad's big announcement," said Suzanne. "Exciting news, isn't it?" she said.

"What news?"

"You haven't heard? Clarissa, get out from behind me! Give your uncle a hug."

She picked up the girl and thrust her into Patrick's arms. Clarissa did not protest. She only cocked her head to one side and pet Patrick's cheek.

"That is the strangest thing. I've never seen her do that. She's not really shy, but you have to push her into things."

"Suzanne, what announcement?"

"It's so hard to stay in a conversation when you have little ones. Rumor has it that your father is going to propose tonight."

"Oh, that. Right."

"Well, gosh, we'd better get in there. We don't want to miss it, do we? Are you going to take Clarissa with you? That'd be such a big help."

Before he could protest, Suzanne had corralled the boys and was shepherding them down the hall. Patrick shifted Clarissa to his hip and followed her mother.

The podium outside the door was abandoned and they let

themselves in. Applause burst forth as they entered and, for a moment, Patrick thought it was he, Suzanne, and the children being applauded for reasons unknown. But as his eyes adjusted, he saw that the entirety of the party was facing away from the door, cheering his father and Marie. The two were holding hands and Marie, smiling, waved the back of her free hand toward her audience. Even from the back of the room, the diamond was impossible to miss.

As the applause rained down, Patrick scanned the crowd until he saw Jack off to his right. He was leaning against the bar, arms crossed, staring intently and without expression at the two figures on the stage.

"Granddad," said Clarissa, pointing toward the stage.

"That's right."

"Uncle Pat," she said, putting her finger on Patrick's chest.

"Right again."

The patriarch held up his hand and the crowd noise ebbed.

"As many of you know, I opened my first market forty-five years ago. Took two years just to turn a profit. But I knew I had something, so the month after we turned our first profit, I bought another market, then another one. We kept pushing, kept growing, and now as I stand here, I can say that Coastal Seafood is the largest family-owned seafood distributor in the Southeast."

There was more applause, but Henry held his hands up impatiently.

"We own thirty-seven seafood markets from Virginia to Florida. We own five major distributorships, a fleet of state-of-the-art fishing vessels, the best crews of fishermen in the world, and a shipping and distribution system that delivers our brand all across the world. No one gets there fresher and no one gets there faster."

Again there was applause, and this time Henry allowed it to continue for a moment before holding up his hands.

"For forty-five years, the Coastal Seafood Company has known only one owner. But we all know that I can't run it forever. Believe it or not, I'm not a young man anymore."

A subdued murmur rose toward the chandeliers, taking with it the jovial mood of the room and replacing it with a general unease, a tense excitement.

Patrick handed Clarissa back to her mother.

"In order to spend more time with my new bride-to-be and to enjoy the fruits of my labor, I've decided to take a step back and bring in a couple of partners."

He made a sweeping gesture toward the side of the room and, on cue, Sean and Bryan took their places alongside their father.

He shook their hands and there was a confused smattering of applause that unified and grew louder only when Henry applauded as well. Patrick looked toward Jack and was not surprised to find Jack watching him.

"Of course, those of you who know me know that I won't give up control that easily. I will maintain a one-third share in the company; Sean and Bryan will each control a third. But, effective immediately, I am leaving the day-to-day operations in the capable hands of my sons, Sean and Bryan.

"Now, some of you may be wondering about my third son, Patrick."

Again there was murmuring in the crowd and Patrick felt warmth rise in his throat. The murmurers turned to find him and he could feel their eyes on him. He did not take his eyes off his father.

"Patrick hasn't shown the same enthusiasm for the family business as his brothers. He's my son, and it was my earnest desire that he take part in the company, so despite his careless attitude, I tried many times to bring him into the fold. But he wasn't interested, and this company has no room for anyone not willing to give it their best. It saddens me to say that Patrick will remain unaffiliated with the company, but it will remain this way until such time as he shows the same dedication as his brothers. But, hell, two out of three ain't bad, right?"

Patrick's pulse quickened. Nothing Henry had said was anything new to Patrick, but he had never heard Henry say it in public before.

Patrick found Jack again, ignored the stares, and mouthed the question, *"What is he doing?"*

Jack shook his head and shrugged, but Patrick could tell that Jack wasn't comfortable either, that it had struck his ear wrong as well.

Patrick turned away. He set Clarissa down next to her brothers.

He left the room lit by chandeliers and nervous laughter and did not slow down until he was at last outside.

He breathed deeply the cool of the night and felt it tight around his face. He felt for his car keys in his pocket. Then, as he had done before, he packed it all together, his father and his brothers, their wives and all the other faces, the fine clothing and the crystal, the sidelong glances and the sounds and the smells of the lobby, the creases beneath his father's eyes inches away from him, and he held all things of the Delacroix inside himself for a moment. And then he let them go.

CHAPTER FIVE

The road was flat and straight and there was very little traffic going to the coast at that hour. Patrick drove without music. The night wore heavy around him and he neither thought about it nor sought to avoid the thoughts. He did not try to make sense of any of it; he neither assigned guilt nor granted lenience. Instead he stared ahead at the lit asphalt before him and the sound of the road enshrouded him and he allowed his mind to drift freely wherever it pleased. The images flitted about as in a dream and he simply drove on while it happened because none of it was new and he knew he needed to allow it to happen.

His thoughts landed on Bryan. He wondered whether Bryan was numb. He wondered whether he felt trapped, whether he was aware of how he was wedged between his father and wife and older brother, whether he hoped or dreamed anything anymore. Or had he switched it all off long ago, or killed it off or had it killed off for him and no longer even considered himself in any of the things he did. Gripping the wheel harder, Patrick hoped Bryan was numb.

Sean was thirteen when Patrick was born and he was already gone. By the time Patrick was aware of his father and his mother and the place they held in the world, Sean was finishing college and already following Henry into the business. Sean's demeanor towards Patrick had always mimicked that of their father, quietly approving when his actions conformed to their standards, noisily objecting when they did not. Sean became what Patrick had always assumed he would become.

But Bryan had been different. He had taught Patrick to throw a baseball as a kid and taken him to his tee-ball games, and some of Patrick's earliest memories were of sitting in the stands with his mother watching Bryan pitch in high school. And he was good. He was tall and lean and strong and he had friends and girls who came by the house on Friday nights. He had a smile.

He was drafted out of high school and played in the minor leagues, but his fastball never consistently broke ninety and his curveball never quite developed a sharp enough break. After three years of hanging around in the minors, it became evident that he was never going to get a real shot at the big leagues. Their father, who had tolerated "this baseball thing" beyond his usual capacity for things he deemed frivolous, pulled the plug. Bryan followed orders. He went to school, then he went to work. He never spoke of baseball again.

Patrick often wondered where it had gone. It didn't seem possible that something so cherished could just go away, vanish into the ether without so much as a shadow of a thought ever again. He wondered if Bryan saw the game when he closed his eyes at night, if he still played when no one was around to tell him not to. He wondered if his sleep was ever interrupted by a spinning white sphere streaked with red flying homeward from the tips of his fingers and, if so, what happened? Did he throw strikes? Did he conquer foes, watch in triumph as his unassailable fastball blew by impotent batsmen?

Or did batters put good wood on the ball? Did he dream of being conquered, of falling short, of watching the ball sail over the fence? Was Bryan bested in his sleep as well?

Patrick's thoughts swung wildly onto the girl; Jennifer. He had known it would happen: he had expected it and he did not fight it. She was willowy.

Willowy.

He had looked the word up after he met her, had sought the word, had dug through a box in the spare bedroom at two in the morning to find a thesaurus to find the word he knew he lacked. But she was gone and would not come back and he would not go find her because he could not offer what she wanted.

It had happened before. It was why he was sure, why this time it hadn't been as hard as the other times. Girls liked him, always had. He was not conceited about it; he was not impressed by it. They liked him because he was quiet and strong and gentle, and probably a little because he didn't try to get them to like him. Yet invariably each relationship came to a point where they wanted more from him, that last bit of whatever it was that he held back, but they were mistaken. He was not holding anything back. It simply was not there. He lacked some vital component of love's mechanics, some small corner of a soul that granted access to another, that allowed someone inside unfettered and unhurt. It wasn't broken, wasn't well-hidden or well-protected, wasn't too small. It just was not there. He didn't have it and he knew it.

Jennifer had gotten closer to him than anyone before her and Patrick had hoped she wouldn't go looking for it, that she didn't need it and that they could find another way, but that's not the way it works. So it was with great sadness but without surprise that he watched her leave.

Five percent.

He laughed to himself without mirth. When she had left, he continued to operate at normal capacity and he estimated that ninety-five percent of the time it didn't bother him. It was the five percent of the time that got to him and, during those times, it stung like hell. When he woke up and the morning was gray and rainy. Sometimes when he looked at the cat which Jennifer had, inexplicably, adored. Always at the very end of the day, but only for a minute or two. And when he drove home from somewhere he never should have gone and had grown sick once more with the certainty that his father would die without anything of any merit ever having passed between them, and the tires on asphalt made a lonely, hollow, empty sound that he could feel in his chest.

Five percent.

From Jennifer came Helen and, once more, he felt a deep, cold sadness for her child, his nephew, who would have a hard life and would never know he wasn't to blame. From Helen and Henry Jr. to Suzanne, and Patrick failed, as he always did, to reconcile the vastness of the gap between the two women. He couldn't fathom how his brothers had married such astonishingly different people. Helen he could understand somewhat; he'd always assumed that she had insisted and that Bryan had followed along. But Suzanne made no sense to him and he could not understand what possible reason she would have had for marrying Sean. Half-formed notions of money and security passed by, but nothing had ever really added up.

On a Thanksgiving several years before, Patrick had confronted Sean. They'd all sat around the dinner table, he and his brothers and their wives and his father. Sean had been poking fun at him the way he and Bryan had done since Patrick was a kid, making fun of how different he looked from the rest of the family, laughing at his size and his hair color and the deep tan of his skin, making semi-obnoxious insinuations about his true lineage. As a child, Patrick had endured their sport without much consternation, but he had always been aware of the difference between Bryan and Sean. Bryan's joking was good-natured; he followed his brother's lead and meant no harm. But Sean's was something else, a point to prove, a surreptitious attempt, though couched in good humor, to let Patrick know where he stood in the pecking order. He would push it as far as he could until their mother called him off.

But on that particular night, with their mother gone, Patrick put an end to it himself. Sean was in mid-sentence when Patrick stood abruptly and hit him. Hard. He squared his shoulders and propelled himself forward from his hips, nearly threw himself across the table with the force of the punch. Sean caught it square on the jaw and his head snapped around, his chin sagged and lolled, and then all of him sagged as he toppled out of the chair.

For a moment, there was no sound at the table beyond the scuffling of a semi-conscious Sean as he tried in vain to pull himself to his feet. But no one was watching Sean. Patrick felt them watching but was distracted by his own lack of anger. It had been a problem of logic. He had stumbled over the sheer absurdity of someone like Sean making fun of someone like him, making fun of the fact that he was large and strong and worked for a living. And he could not find words to express the absurdity, so the physical reaction had shot out of him, had rectified the imbalance. As he stood over his brother, he felt for the first time an inkling of his action being wrong, or perhaps right, or of any moral or ethical value whatsoever. He looked down at his glassy-eyed brother and left the room.

There had been no repercussions, nothing concrete anyway. When he returned to the house hours later, Sean had left and no one who remained said anything. No one ever spoke of the incident and, had Sean not spent the next six weeks with his jaw wired together, Patrick would have wondered if it had happened at all. The only discernible change was that, from that point on, he could always get Sean to back away from him, if the need arose, by even the slightest gesture toward a physical threat. It was not a tactic Patrick enjoyed employing, but he liked knowing it was there if he ever needed it.

He drove on and as he turned off the interstate onto the local highway that ran close to the main part of town, a fire blazed in his mind. It reached toward the sky and billowed thick, black smoke high into the air and he saw it as he had seen it years before, could feel the heat dry his forehead and glow in the tears on his cheek.

It was the night after his mother died. He returned to the house that would be his, looked around and saw the relics of his mother's illness and did not stop to think about it. He took all of it, the wheelchair and the canes, the rows of medications from the cabinet, the books she had read toward the end, the bedside table and the glass of water that sat on it, the safety railing he'd installed in the shower. He took things he perhaps ought not have taken, clothes and things someone may have wanted, but he took it all the same, and piled all of it high on the driveway. Finally, he dragged the bed itself out the door and forced it atop the pile.

He poured gasoline on it and struck the match.

The firemen found him standing alone in his driveway, silhouetted by the glow, staring into the flames. They didn't say anything. They knew who he was, and it was not difficult to figure out what he had done. Eventually, one of them put an arm around his shoulders and led him away. Patrick followed without protest as the others put the fire out. They didn't bother with citations or warnings.

The one who had led him from the fire asked if he needed anything, if there was anyone they could call. Patrick, slumped on the porch step with his head resting on the railing, shook his head. The firemen hung around for a good while and no one talked.

Patrick had always been grateful to them for having stayed. His was not a world of cruelty, but it often lacked kindness as well. The night gathered itself a little tighter around him and he missed his mother, who had been kind.

There had been another O'Reilly sibling. She was born four years before Patrick. They named her Mary after her maternal grandmother and she lived for twenty-three hours and thirty-eight minutes. A congenital heart defect could not support a life but allowed her almost a full day. Mary O'Reilly had not been expected to survive her birth; the doctors had been surprised that the stress of delivery hadn't rendered her a stillborn.

Her father called her a "fighter." It was the highest compliment he knew how to give; he, who could not define family without loss. She had her day, just long enough to make a father proud. Just long enough to breathe in the air that sustains all life. Just long enough for her mother to smell her head.

Henry took his two young sons to the hospital to see Mary when she was born. He knew that she would not live but he wanted his sons to meet their sister. Patrick did not know whether or not the visit had been traumatic for the boys, whether they had felt the loss or comprehended it all, or whether they even remembered it.

For Patrick, his sister existed only in an ethereal state. Each year, on Mary's birthday, the family gathered around the dinner table and his mother said a prayer for her. It was always a quiet dinner and it was the only day during the year when everyone was certain to be present. As a child, Patrick had found nothing unusual about the annual event. It was just something that was done. As he grew older, however, the day created a distance between he and the rest of his family. It was nothing manifest; nobody ever mentioned the fact that he was the only one who had never seen his sister. Yet with each passing year, he felt more and more like an uninvited guest whom everyone was too polite to ask to leave.

He had always had the impression that he was something of a consolation prize to his mother, perhaps not exactly an attempt to recreate the past but at least an effort to put a seal on what would otherwise be an ever growing string of empty years trailing backward from Mary's death. He wondered whether his father had to be talked into having another child, whether either parent was disappointed that he wasn't a girl. He had never felt like a replacement child. It was more as if he was corrective in some way, an attempt to balance the loss of a life by creating a new one, like planting a tree where another had been cut down.

Patrick turned down the road leading to his house and was startled to realize that he had no recollection of having driven through town. He pulled into his driveway, where the headlights found the charred spot on the concrete that could not be cleaned and would not fade. He sat for a long time with the engine running, staring first at the black spot, then off into the darkness over the water.

He backed out of the driveway. He drove through the sleeping town to the highway and turned onto the road that led to the bridge to Watchman's Island.

CHAPTER SIX

The South Bar was less a bar than two mobile homes pushed together with a crudely made plywood bar top in the middle where the shared walls had once been. It was unclear whether it was called the South Bar because it was situated near the southernmost part of Watchman's Island or because it was in the South and featured a forlorn-looking Confederate flag draped about the heavily smudged mirror behind the bar.

Aside from the flag, there was not much in the way of adornment. Neon lights featuring various beer brands hung from the wall, a lopsided Atlanta Braves pennant was mounted over the door, and a well-used jukebox stood in the corner. In front of the jukebox was a square of faux-wood parquet that served as a dance floor. A few tables with mismatched chairs were scattered around, and that was it.

It was a locals' bar. Tourists rarely ventured inside, owing in part to the fact that it appeared to be a rougher bar than it was, but mostly because it didn't, upon first glance, look like an operating business at all. It looked like a pair of abandoned mobile homes sitting on a gravel lot. The occasional handful of tourists who did venture inside typically took a quick look around and left. Every once in a while, a group of wayward middle-aged boating types or heavily-besotted spring break kids came and stayed for a drink but they spent most of their time attempting to appear casual while peering around apprehensively. Fishermen drank comfortably at the South Bar, as did construction guys and tradesmen and local women trying to find fishermen or construction guys or tradesmen to either sleep with or marry or some sort of arrangement in between.

Not even the smell of stale beer in still air had changed since Patrick had last set foot in the bar. It was a hole in the world free from evolution, a vinyl-encased exception to the passage of time. But the stasis of the bar was of comfort to Patrick as he took a seat. Two old men sat at the elbow of the bar clutching bottles of beer in their weather-clawed hands and stared listlessly at a television that hung from the ceiling.

"Look at these two barnacles," said Patrick from his seat beside them. "Nobody's scraped you off yet?"

The man closest to Patrick looked at him blankly, then nudged his mate.

"Hey, Frank, look at this. Some smart-mouth kid took a wrong turn over the bridge and wound up here. Guess he figures on pestering a couple of old men trying to drink a beer."

His partner looked over, then back at the TV.

"Naw. He's in the right place. Just the wrong time. Reckon that wedding party isn't 'til tomorrow. No, wait. Maybe he's our waiter. Maybe that's why he's dressed like that."

"Yeah, right. Like either of you old bastards have ever been to that kind of restaurant."

The two men cackled. The one closest to Patrick gripped him by the shoulder and gave it a shake.

"Patrick O'Reilly. How you been, son?"

"Not too bad. You?"

"Doin' good. Just been ridin' this here trusty vessel," said Artie. He slapped the top of the bar and Frank chuckled.

"Catching anything out there?" asked Patrick.

Both men grumbled in unison.

"Nothing worth a damn, that's for sure," said Artie.

"Ain't like it used to be," said Frank.

"So here's what I don't get," said Patrick. "I've been asking about the catch for something like twenty years. And for twenty years, you've been complaining about it. If that's the case, why the hell are you still in the game? Matter of fact, how can you afford to stay in the game?"

"Well, now, just what the hell else would I do with myself all day?" asked Artie.

"Tell you what, Patrick," said Frank. "You should've seen it out there years ago. Could've scooped the fish out with a bucket. Could've caught all you want sittin' here at the bar. Ain't the same these days."

Frank shook his head slowly and Patrick waited as the two old pairs of eyes walked a silent tired path to the past. Frank came back first.

"Hey, that your boat I've seen tied up at that new place on the sound?" he said.

"Yeah, that's me."

"One hell of a goddamn house, ain't it? And that lawn. Looks like a damn golf course."

"I'll tell you what," chimed in Artie, "it's one goddamn mansion after another these days. You remember what it used to be like on the south side of the island?"

"You mean before I was born? No, I don't remember that," said Patrick.

"Wiseass," said Artie. "Sometimes I forget you're a young turd. You walk around this place like an old man trying to hide from your wife."

"You should have seen it, Patrick," said Frank, picking up Artie's dropped thread. "Folks used to live in these little houses, look like shacks compared to what they got now. 'Bungalows,' that's the word. That's what people would call them now. 'Bungalows.' Hell, we just called them houses. You'd have your house, and a little yard, and on it would go, rows of these houses and people who knew their neighbors. Ain't like that now. Now you got these houses on the ocean side jammed together to where you can just about reach out one window and touch your neighbor's house. And they're all on stilts and two or three stories high so you can barely see the water from the road. And on the sound side? Forget about it. All mansions with big green yards that stretch out forever. Like that one you're working on, Pat. What's the name of that family?"

"Porter."

"Porter. Never heard of 'em. See what I mean? You used to know people around here."

"Frank, you live on the north side," said Patrick.

"Yeah, so?"

"And you've always lived on the north side, right?"

"All my life," said Frank.

"Well, then, why do you give a damn what they've done with the south side? If anything, all these weekend places and houses for retired rich folks are going to boost your property value. Hell, you could sell your house right now and retire a rich man."

"I don't know. It used to be different, that's all. People used to know each other. People used to give a damn about each other, back when both sides of the island were the same.

"I'll tell you what. That storm came through here and just knocked the piss out of everyone. Split this place in two. And not just the island itself. I mean it split all of us in two. It's like a bunch of money blew in with the storm and all of it landed on the south side."

"You got to admit that was some smart business," said Artie.

Frank nodded. Disappointment sagged around Patrick; he knew where the conversation would turn.

"Buying up all that land from folks who couldn't stand to live there no more," said Artie. "Folks who lost everything they had, didn't want to stick around and rebuild. Or couldn't afford to. Probably got it for pretty cheap too. I'm sure he got himself a deal."

"And that channel, too," added Frank, nodding in the direction of the water that lay not far beyond the wall of the bar. "We'd have been lost without that. You know all about that, right, Pat?"

"I do."

"Francesca damn near destroyed Spring Tide," said Frank, undaunted by Patrick's response. "Wasn't just the island that got hit. When that storm came through and cut the island in half, it dumped a whole bunch of sand in the channel. Or, at least, where the channel used to be. The old channel ain't nothing more than a creek now. Barely get a johnboat through it at high tide. Point of the story is that Spring Tide lost its channel out to the ocean. A fishing town with no access to the ocean ain't much of a town.

"A lot of people got hit hard on the mainland. Lot of people left town. But the mayor and his pals, pretty much everyone really, kind of just wrung their hands. It would take years to dredge out the channel again, they said. And forget about the cost. It would have bankrupted the town before it could start to save it."

"Yep, your father did a hell of a lot for this place," said Artie. "It was his idea, you know. Dredging out behind the new inlet the storm had made. All they really had to do was connect the sound to the town docks. And he paid for the whole damn thing out of his own pocket. And bear in mind, he wasn't as . . . Well, he was doing fine, don't get me wrong, but it wasn't like it is with him now. It's not like he had that much cash just lying around.

"He didn't ask permission, either. Just up and did it. One day these barges showed up and started dragging out the mud and sand. I guess your dad figured that by the time anyone got the mind to stop him, it'd already be done. He was right, too."

"Tell you what," said Frank, reclaiming his narrative from Artie, "the mayor was some kind of pissed. It made him look bad. Like he'd been standing around with his thumb up his ass while the town starved to death. But what was done was done. They'd have hung him in the streets if he'd tried to close that channel. I guess it didn't matter, though.

He wasn't mayor for much longer after that."

"What a surprise," said Patrick.

"You know, Pat," said Frank. "Everyone's got their opinion but, for my money, no one's done more for this place than your dad. I don't think we would have survived without him."

Patrick nodded. He had argued the point before and had gotten nowhere and he was not going to try again. He would nod and wait until they spoke of something else. He felt tired and it was not because of the late hour.

Artie and Frank, however, had reached the end of their tale and ceased their duet. The noise of the bar rose around the men as they turned their eyes back to the dusty television. Patrick drank his beer and listened to the old men periodically grunt in approval or derision at whatever was on the screen.

"Ha!" came a voice from behind Patrick. "Look who's made his triumphant return to this fine establishment!"

Patrick turned to find Davis Osterlin staring at him, and the rest of the bar's patrons staring at Davis, whose voice had always been a little more boisterous than his narrow frame indicated. Unabashed, Davis stood in the doorway, grinning in mock astonishment with his arms flung wide. Patrick shook his head and smiled as the patrons resumed their activities and Davis made his way toward him.

When most of their peers had left for college, Davis had wandered off to the Pacific Northwest. No one was quite sure where he had gone or what he was doing on the opposite side of the continent, but when he came back three years later, there was a firmness to his grip and a sharpness in his eye that hadn't been there before. He was still easy of manner and quick to laugh, but he had lost the goofy softness that had been there before. He was the only friend Patrick had kept from high school.

"You may be a tad overdressed," said Davis as he settled onto a barstool next to Patrick. "How embarrassing for you."

"I don't think you're in the right place, Davis. I don't see any freshman girls anywhere around here waiting to be preyed upon by a pretend college professor."

"And people say you have no sense of humor," said Davis. "If you must know, I've come here to lay low. And if you're dismayed to see me, just wait until you see who's with me. I believe he's in the parking lot on his phone, desperately trying to avoid laying low."

"No."

"Oh, yes."

"Honestly. Why do you still hang out with that guy? Don't you find him a little much?"

"I find him a source of great comedy," said Davis. "Even if much of that comedy is inadvertent."

The door swung open and Karl Swardson stepped in. He made a quick survey of the room, then marched toward Davis with a wrinkled nose and a scowl.

"What the fuck is this?" said Karl. "What are we doing here? We could've been in Wilmington. No girl is ever, ever going to come out here to the sticks to hang out in this dump."

Patrick, who was facing the bar and away from Karl, made an apologetic wave toward Artie and Frank. The gesture caught Karl's eye and arrested his momentum.

"Oh, shit!" said Karl. "Pat O'Reilly! Damn!"

Patrick warded off a hug with a forearm and the two settled on an awkward handshake.

"Shit, man, how long's it been?" asked Karl.

"A good while," said Patrick.

He and Karl had been close friends in middle school, but Patrick's sentiment toward him had played out in indirect proportion to his friendship with Davis. Karl's father was a prominent defense attorney and, as such, Karl felt that he and Patrick were members of some form of elite fraternity. Patrick acknowledged no such bond, and the stronger the association in Karl's mind became, the farther Patrick drifted from him.

"So, any girls come through here?" Karl asked Patrick.

"Ever? Or tonight?" asked Davis.

"Tonight, man! What the fuck? I'm trying to get laid."

"If you're just 'trying to get laid,'" said Davis, "and you don't care about specifics, then you'll be best advised to pick one of the gentlemen in here."

"Ha ha. Very funny," said Karl.

"Funny, hell! I'm serious. In absolute values, the guys in here are probably more good-looking than the women," said Davis. "If you're not particular."

"Whatever," said Karl. "Anyway, all I'm saying is we could have gone to Wilmington tonight. We could leave right now, matter of fact. Get there in time for last call. Pick up all the drunk bitches."

"Have you ever considered that your success rate would be much higher if you didn't insist on calling them 'bitches'?" asked Davis.

"Hey, nothing wrong with my success rate," said Karl, puffing out his chest a bit.

"And yet, here we sit," said Davis.

"Whatever, man. Just because you're around all those college bitches all the time," said Karl. He turned to Patrick. "So, what's with the tux?"

"Yes, Patrick. What's with the tux?" said Davis, leaning forward.

"You know full well why I'm wearing this."

"I do not!" said Davis. He shrugged his shoulders in mock innocence and Patrick gave him a withering glare. "Was it, perhaps, a party of some kind?"

"It was."

"And for whom was this party held? Was it a wedding reception?"

"No."

"A fund raiser?"

"You know it wasn't."

"A gala event? Book release party? Yacht commissioning?"

"You know this is just going to set him off," said Patrick.

Karl, who lacked the intellectual curiosity necessary to maintain a sure grasp of subtlety, had lost interest in the conversation and was actively scanning and re-scanning the bar for phantom women.

"Would it really?" asked Davis. "How would it set him off? Why would the mention of your having attended one of your father's world-renowned parties interest him at all?"

"Wait," said Karl. He snapped back into the conversation and held an arm out in front of Patrick as if to detain the stationary man. "Your father had a party tonight? That's where you were?"

Patrick nodded. Davis' eyes widened in anticipation.

"Oh, man! Shit, man! I have got to get into one of those. I mean, I've heard those things are the parties of the century. What the fuck, Pat? How come you never take me?"

"I don't usually bring a date."

"Man. If I could just get into one of those. You have no idea. You should have called me."

"What difference could it possibly make to you?"

"Well, you know," said Karl. Uncertainty crossed his brow but sank beneath the next wave of bravado. "Everyone who's anyone goes to those things. The networking you could do there—you'd be a millionaire by the next day. Stocks, real estate, investment banking. All kinds of things you could get into."

"It's mostly people in the restaurant business," said Patrick.

"Oh, bullshit," bellowed Karl. "You think I don't know what kind of people your father hangs out with? You think I don't know? I'm not talking about hanging out with his employees and fucking Joe Fisherman."

"You better take it easy in here with that," said Patrick.

"Whatever. I'm just saying. If I could just get in there," he said again, shaking his head wistfully.

"Oh, honestly. What would you do, supposing you got yourself invited?" said Davis. "Assuming you passed the requisite security checks, the bouncers and plain-clothes police that work the crowd, and the bomb-sniffing dogs? Once inside, with the three-story ice sculptures that spout champagne and the choir of vestal virgins and the waitresses that float about the room suspended by wires, what would you do? Would you know to whom to bow? Who to greet first? Who prefers a handshake to a kiss on the ring? And once you're shoulder to shoulder with all those captains of industry, what would you say to them? What would you have gained by mere fact of your presence?"

"I don't know. I mean, what the hell? I'm just saying it'd be cool as shit to go," said Karl, finally arriving at the conclusion that he was being made fun of.

"Well, I'm sure you're right. I'm sure it would be 'cool as shit.'"

"Anyway, I bet my father was there," said Karl with a shrugging attempt at recouping some sense of casual coolness.

"Didn't see him there," said Patrick, eliciting a poorly suppressed snort from Davis.

"Yeah, I'll have to ask him tomorrow if he went. I mean, he's gone to tons of those parties. Obviously. You know, as far back as our fathers go and all. Of course he'd be invited. I think my dad represented your dad once a long time ago as a matter of fact."

"Nope," said Patrick.

"Well, it would've been years ago."

"Nope," said Patrick. "You just made that up. To sound cool."

"Well, how do you know? It could have been when we were kids. It could have been before we were born."

"Because," said Patrick, "for one thing, my father has his own lawyers, and he is their only client. And my brother is his head counsel. My father owns his company in a way that you've never owned anything in your life. There is no facet of it that he doesn't rule over obsessively. There is no length he wouldn't go to protect himself and his assets, including more or less buying a town piece by piece and getting his own personal sheriff elected. So, the odds against anyone in this county, from the District Attorney down, pressing charges against him are staggering even if he, for some reason, committed a crime that anyone would ever find out about. So there is no fucking way he would ever need an ambulance-chasing TV-commercial lawyer like your father. Not now. Not when we were kids. And not before we were born. No one gives a shit about you or your dad. So do us all a favor and drink your beer and shut the fuck up."

There was silence. Patrick's neck and face grew warm. As he turned back to the bar and put both elbows on it, he noticed Davis' raised eyebrows. He could feel Karl behind him, sorting out what had been said, trying to salvage his bent pride. He could feel Karl inching toward a mistake so he kept his elbows on the bar and turned a pint glass around and around with his thumb and middle finger and waited and hoped it wouldn't happen.

"Jesus, man," said Karl, "you don't have to be such a prick about it."

"All right, Karl. Let's drop it," said Davis.

"You drop it, Davis," said Karl, and Patrick could hear his recklessness. "He doesn't need to be talking about my dad like that."

"All right," said Davis. "Take it easy. I'm sure he didn't really mean anything by that. Let's get another round."

"He doesn't get to say whatever he wants just because of who he is," Karl said.

Patrick spun around on his stool.

"What's that mean, because of who I am? What do you mean by that?"

"He's just a little hot, Pat. He wasn't saying anything," said Davis.

"You know damn well what I mean," said Karl, thoroughly disinterested in the lifeline Davis had tried to throw him. "You think because everyone knows your last name you can say whatever you want and everyone will just get out of your way."

"You don't know what you're talking about."

"The hell I don't. Everyone in this town knows it."

"Karl, I'm warning you. You need to shut your mouth."

"You don't get to tell me what to do!" shouted Karl, hot-faced and high-pitched. "We shouldn't be doing this. People like us—"

Patrick's arm shot out from his body. The glass fell from his grip and, before it could shatter on the floor, his hand had cinched around Karl's throat. Though he remained seated, his palm struck Karl's throat with such force that Karl would have fallen over backwards had it not been for Patrick's grip. Karl's eyes bulged and his hands grasped desperately, futilely, at Patrick's arm.

"'People like us'?" Patrick growled. "What do you mean, '*people like us*'? You mean rich snobs who think they're better than everyone? Is that what you mean? Is that who I am?"

Karl did not respond; his eyes were locked on Patrick in white-rimmed terror. A frantic hissing sputtered from his lips along with a fine spray as he struggled to breathe. The muscles on Patrick's forearm bulged taut and unforgiving and with his free hand he swatted away Karl's flailing attempts to both push him away and pull himself free.

You let him go. You have to and you know it.

You could just squeeze.

He's not the problem.

Patrick saw only the red, desperate face. There was no periphery. Then he saw Davis' hand on his wrist, his face in front of Karl's. Davis did not speak, did not attempt to pull Patrick's hand free. He looked Patrick in the eye and kept his hand on Patrick's wrist.

"Not in here," said Frank from behind him. "You're not doing that in here." Patrick felt strong hands on his shoulder and around his waist. Finally, he released his grip as Frank and Artie pulled him away.

Karl collapsed onto the floor and held his blanched throat with both hands. His breath came in a heaving rattle and spit covered his chin and dribbled onto his chest. He did not try to speak and he did not look at Patrick as Davis knelt beside him and tried to get him to his feet.

"I'm sorry," Patrick mumbled to no one in particular and too quietly for Karl to hear.

He turned and, ducking under the weight of the shocked, silent stares that followed him, left the bar and slammed the door behind him.

CHAPTER SEVEN

It was a quiet night and the sound of the waves rushing onto the shore was strangely magnified by the silence. It was not loud but it was all-encompassing; the ocean's sound carried through the air and filled the space around Patrick. In the empty night, it sounded hollow and eternal and omnipresent even though Patrick could not see the ocean past the row of beach front houses.

He was walking toward the southernmost point of the island for no reason other than that it was an attainable point not too far off. He could still feel the warmth on his face and on the back of his neck, and he felt as if his ears were ringing from the noise of the bar even though it had not been loud. His heart was still beating too fast and a bitter taste remained in the back of his dry throat. He walked along quietly and listened to the metronome ocean off in the darkness to his left.

He stopped when he ran out of road and looked out at the calm of the channel. His gaze swept across the water and, from his vantage point, he could almost see his entire world. Off to his left the ocean, tamed by a breakwater, calmed itself as it became the channel that wrapped around the southern point of the island where he stood. To his right, down the channel and past the marsh, Spring Tide glowed in the distance.

The water twinkled in the night and the darkness seemed to move around him like the flattening, widening ripples on a pond after the surface has been disturbed. The water calmed him; he suspected he had known it would. He stared out across the channel at the now-uninhabited island to the south that had once been a part of the land upon which he stood, and the sound of the water mesmerized him and he closed his eyes, kept them closed until he heard someone approaching.

"Why do you stay here?" asked Davis as he joined him in looking out upon the channel and island beyond.

"Where would I go?"

"I don't know. Anywhere. It seems to me there are a few thousand miles of coastline in this country that could use docks. Or you could do something else."

"I guess," said Patrick.

"So why do you stay in this town?"

"Because I live here too, that's why. The hell with him."

The two men stood in silence for a while, both with hands in pockets, both staring out at the water.

"How is he?" asked Davis. "How are things between the two of you?"

"Same," said Patrick.

"So the old man's still thinking you'll take up the family business."

"Yeah."

"And you're not going to do that."

"Nope."

"Well, I can certainly see how that's something of an impasse."

"I just don't understand it," said Patrick. "He's got Bryan and Sean. What does he need me for?"

"He just wants the complete set. Or he can't handle someone telling him no. Or there's the other possibility."

"Which is?"

"He wants to make sure you'll be taken care of."

"I doubt that's it."

"Of course you do," said Davis, "but think about it. He's not a young man. By this point, I'm sure he's considered the end. You don't think he'd like to have all his ducks in a row?"

"I think it's a lot more likely that he's worried more about his company than he is about me."

Davis opened his mouth to respond but said nothing. Silence eased its way back around them. At night on the water, silence is the natural state of things; conversations take root only by intention. It is difficult to have an awkward silence along a darkened shore. Water at night smothers insignificant chatter, or at least renders it artificial.

"My father's getting old," Patrick said, so suddenly that he startled Davis.

"Why do you say that?"

Patrick remembered something. "It's hard to describe. He just seems a little off."

"How so?"

"He couldn't remember Jennifer's name. Or he remembered it wrong. He told Jack her name was Jessica."

"So? Had he ever met her?"

Patrick shook his head.

"You don't understand. He doesn't forget names. Ever. It's a point of pride for him as a businessman. But there's other stuff too."

"Like what?"

"I don't know. Hard to say. He just seemed a little off, that's all. It's probably just me. I hadn't seen him in a while."

"Well, he is, as you mentioned, getting older. Anyone else notice anything? What about your brothers?"

"Don't think so."

"So, what are you going to do?"

"I don't know. Nothing, I guess," said Patrick. Uneasiness came over him unexpectedly, a strange sense of time passing without him, a missed something somewhere inside that he could neither identify nor reconcile. He felt as if he had been running for a long time with his head down and, having finally looked up, realized he didn't know where he was.

"Is Karl all right?" he asked, jerking his head in the direction of the bar.

Davis flicked a wrist in front of him as if shooing away a mosquito.

"Bruised ego. He'll be fine," Davis said. "You've no idea how often someone takes a swing at that guy. He is a bit of an ass."

"And you just let him take a beating?"

"Does he look like he's missing any teeth? Come on, Patrick. You know me better than that. I knew you wouldn't really hurt him."

"I could have," he said. "I could have hurt him bad. And that wasn't even about him. Karl's an ass all right, but he didn't deserve that."

Davis shrugged. "It's not as if he was standing there minding his own business," he said. "He'll be fine."

"Where is he? Where'd he go?"

"He's in the car. Pouting. Probably making wild claims to himself about what he'll do to you next time he sees you."

"Not likely to hear any of that myself, am I?" asked Patrick.

"I would think not," said Davis with a smile. "Hey, do you remember that time when we were kids and we got caught shoplifting at that gas station?"

"I don't think 'we' got caught shoplifting so much as you and your friend got caught shoplifting and I got caught being with you guys."

"Fair enough," said Davis. "Then do you remember when we were in high school and you, Karl, and I drove out here that one night raging drunk and got caught trying to drive a truck onto the dunes?"

"Of course."

"You remember who was driving?"

"I was."

"You remember what the cop did?"

"Sure. Made us leave the car and walk home. It was almost dawn when we got to my house. My mother was pissed."

"Sure she was. She was so pissed at you she was pissed at me. You remember when Karl drove his car into that telephone pole and damn near killed me?"

"I wasn't with you guys that night."

"But you knew about it, right?"

"Of course. The whole school did."

"Do you know how drunk he was that night?"

"No. I didn't know he'd been drinking."

"How would you? It's not like he got arrested. Now, let me ask you this: Do you really think a cop would just forget to do a sobriety test on two kids who nearly killed themselves in an accident? Do you think it's standard protocol to allow three obviously drunk teens to get away with drunk driving? To let them leave the car and walk home?"

"What's your point?"

"My point, Patrick, is that Karl wasn't wrong."

"Get the hell out of here."

"You might not like it, but it's true. You and your family don't have the same rules as everybody else. Refusing membership to the club doesn't change that."

"What's your *point*?" Patrick said again.

"You don't get to dictate how the people around you respond to you. And the fact of the matter is that people in this town treat you differently than they do everyone else."

"That's horseshit," said Patrick, though not without doubt.

"Oh, come on. The way you used to tear up this town, you never thought it was strange that you never got so much as a parking ticket?"

A knot was forming in Patrick's stomach. The truth hung over him like the night. His friend was right and he knew it but he fought it nonetheless.

"Patrick," said Davis, his tone softening, "you can't tell me you've never thought about this before."

"I swear I haven't," said Patrick. "It's a small town so I just assumed, you know, we all know each other. I never thought of myself as different. Christ, Davis, why did you bring this up?"

"As much as you seem to think that you're all square with the people in this town, you're not. You never will be. Your father is directly responsible for the welfare of half of them. Probably more than that. When he's gone, the people will turn to you. They're going to look to you to make sure they can pay their mortgages and feed their children and put their kids through school. And not one person is going to give half a damn whether or not you and the old man got along."

"There's Sean and Bryan for all that."

"Yeah, right. No one knows them. You're a local. You're the one they're going to look to for answers and you'd better have something to give them when they do. You can't keep pretending you're just another working stiff. You are who you are, Patrick. You can't let these people down."

Patrick looked across the water to the distant glow of Spring Tide. He had never considered himself anything other than part of the town. But he had never considered himself in any sort of leadership capacity, either. A dense fatigue filled the space the adrenaline had left vacant as it dissipated. He knew Davis was right and it annoyed him but there was no more anger.

"This is all so easy for you," said Patrick, "If you care so much, why don't you get involved? Why don't you do something?"

"Because my name isn't O'Reilly. Because my father sells insurance and no one gives a damn what I have to say."

Patrick looked at him for a hard moment, then stared back out at the stone gray of the water and watched the moon's reflection on the surface as it distorted and came apart. Davis put a hand on his shoulder and, when he spoke again, his voice was hushed and gentle.

"Look," he said, "I know it's not fair. But you can't stay here and be only half of who you are. And if you left, there'd be only half of you wherever you went."

"So where does that leave me?"

Davis shrugged. "It's your home," he said.

Patrick took one last glance out over the water, then walked back to the bar with his friend.

CHAPTER EIGHT

Patrick awoke in the still-dark morning and got dressed. In his half-asleep and slightly hung-over state, the previous night's activities seemed hazy and somehow less real, as if a translucent film separated him from the things he had so recently seen and heard and done. He walked the length of his dock in the damp flat stillness of the morning and dropped his tools into the bottom of the boat. He motored through the mist on a rising tide and found his workers waiting on the unfinished dock, looking confused.

Patrick's crew consisted of two Hispanic men who were cousins. Javier was the elder of the two and spoke little English. José spoke almost none. Patrick spoke little Spanish, but the three of them had devised a system where Patrick and Javier conversed in a terse pidgin that covered all the pertinent aspects of water and carpentry and the relationship between the two. Javier translated to José as needed. The three men knew their jobs well and, with the exception of the intricate dance needed to direct the crane to drive the heavy pilings into the mud, there wasn't all that much that needed to be said.

"Gazebo?" asked Javier. He drew the shape in the air with his hands. "Gazebo, no?"

"No," said Patrick as he tied up. "No. Gazebo mañana. My fault. I didn't finish yesterday."

"We go home?" asked Javier.

"If you want, you can," said Patrick. "Or you can stay. Your call. Trabaja or no. You decide."

Javier translated to José. Both men looked back at Patrick. He knew they wouldn't insist on staying; they wouldn't interfere with the work they knew their boss preferred to do alone. But he also knew they wanted to work and would only speak up if they wanted the day off.

"Hammers, nails," he said to Javier. "We'll set the saw up over here where I stopped yesterday."

The men got to work. Javier and José carried the lumber out to the dock from dry land, measured it, cut it, and brought it to the unfinished edge, where Patrick nailed the boards in place. The three men fell into a familiar, wordless rhythm. The cousins were nearly too fast for Patrick, who could scarcely finish nailing a board down before a new one landed at his feet.

Patrick's arm swung, hammer hit nail, the saw shrieked to life, then faded away behind him. The sweat beaded on his brow, the sun warmed his shoulders, and he found his home out at the end of an unfinished dock the way he always did. The dock was a place of known variables for him; it was a simple question with a simple answer, a place that required no extraneous thought. And it was reasonably safe. There was no way for anyone to inadvertently wander out to where he worked, or to feign a chance encounter as a pretense toward other ends. Men worked out there, and worked a job Patrick understood.

The hammer swung over and over and his stomach began to unclench. He felt the muscles between his shoulder blades unkink and slide easily over one another as the previous day shed its weight and passed over and away from him like a spent cloud. He knew it would come back, not the previous day but a new one. He had hoped it would not be that day, but he knew it would be soon. And he knew the next time would be different, different than any of the encounters he'd had with his father. It would be different, and something inside him that he could not define and would not search for told him it would be worse.

But perched on a narrow wooden ledge between wind and water, he was at home, and he paid for the right to be there with the salt that drained from him into the salt that surrounded him. His father had paid him nothing in a long, long time and Patrick felt superior to him in that regard. The working end of the unfinished dock was his domain and the weight of his family and the ominous portent of their movements, though still present, were as irrelevant and ineffectual as the laws of a foreign country.

The sweat dripped from him now in a steady rhythm under a near-vertical sun. The sweat fell in unceasing sacrifice to the wood and mud below him and in so doing cleansed him, purged from him the alcohol and ill-will of the prior night. The rhythm of his toil was a substitute for thought and, in his ritual of sweat and toil, he found salvation. It was temporary. It always was.

Eventually, the lengthening shadows in the reeds and the sidelong glances of the men told him that the day had come to a close. They packed up and, once Javier and José had left, he stood at the edge of the now-completed dock with his arms crossed. There was more to do, more to add, but the dock was now a dock, and as he turned to look back down the long, straight line of it, he heard a car pull into the driveway. He knew it would be Jack again. He had hoped for more time but, with a heavy sigh, made his way toward the car all the same.

He had hoped for a few days, maybe even weeks. That was the pattern. An argument, a period of silence, a stilted attempt at reconciliation that often rekindled the argument because even Henry O'Reilly's attempts to make peace were uncompromising and hard and directed at, rather than offered to, the aggrieved. But for the silence to end after only a day was an unusual occurrence and Patrick felt cheated out of his rest period.

Jack was leaning against the car waiting for him when Patrick made it to the driveway. He got into the car without a word and Jack did the same. They drove along the shore, over the bridge, through the town, and had turned onto the highway and were headed toward Wilmington before Patrick broke the silence.

"Doesn't it usually take him a few days?"

Jack shook his head.

"This isn't about that," said Jack. "There's something going on that I don't understand."

The hair on Patrick's neck stood up.

"What is it?"

"With your father. And the company. I can't put my finger on it. There are signs, some telltale things. An unusual report from an accountant, a strange call from one of our lawyers. I don't know. Something's off."

"So where are we going?"

"To a meeting."

"What meeting?"

"At the office. With your father and brothers and the rest of the board."

"Jack, what could this possibly have to do with me?"

"You're his son."

"I don't have anything to do with Coastal Seafood. You know that."

"Well, I don't know what this thing is. And until I find out, you're involved. You're his son."

A thought occurred to Patrick, a sinking, worrisome thought.

"He didn't send for me, did he, Jack?" he asked. "He doesn't know I'm coming?"

"No," said Jack. "Your inclusion was my decision."

"So you're taking me, uninvited, to a meeting at his office, after business hours. Jack, what the hell is going on?"

"I honestly don't know. That's why we're going."

They turned where the road ended at the river and headed downtown. Jack pulled into his spot underneath a sprawling old warehouse that had been converted into the headquarters of Coastal Seafood Company. The building was alongside the river but it was no longer a working dock. The once-vibrant pier that ran the length of the building now sagged listlessly over the water and was no longer safe to walk on. The red-brick building itself was weatherworn and faded but the interior had been completely gutted and remodeled. From the inside, it was indistinguishable from any other modern office building apart from the spectacular view overlooking the river and the bridge in the distance.

Jack swiped a card at a rear door and the two men entered. They wound their way through a large room of darkened cubicles toward a stairway, up the stairs to the second floor, and down a hallway of closed doors toward a door at the end of hall. It was the only door from which light was visible where the door met the carpet. Jack opened the door without breaking stride and Patrick followed him in.

Henry O'Reilly stood at the head of a long table that took up most of the small meeting room. The table was situated in the room such that when Jack and Patrick entered, they found themselves staring Henry directly in the face, and it was a long moment before Patrick broke from Henry's gaze and looked down at the other seated figures. On his father's right side were Doug Castin, Sean, Helen, and the newly-engaged Marie. Across the table on Henry's left sat Bryan and three men in suits whom Patrick did not recognize.

The room fell silent upon their entry. The eyes of all seated at the table stared up at the interlopers. Henry stiffened, stared at Jack for a moment, then made a quick hand gesture toward Doug. Doug, who had stopped writing upon the intrusion, put the pen down and closed his notebook.

"How did you know we were here?" asked Henry.

"I know everything that happens inside this building," said Jack.

"Well then, someone in this room has just lost their job." He cast a withering glance around the table. No one met his glare. "I just don't know who it is yet. But then again, it doesn't particularly matter who told you, Jack. What's done is done. And you," he said, jabbing a finger at Patrick, "what the hell are you doing here? Suddenly taking an interest? Now that some ownership is being given out, now that there's a little money in the mix, you come here with your hand out?"

"He came because I brought him here," said Jack. "He didn't know about any of this."

"And why is that?" asked Henry. "Why did you bring him here?"

"Because he's your son, Henry."

"Is he?" asked Henry, derision radiating from him. "Is he really? He's had nothing but chances, Jack. You know that as well as I do. He doesn't want anything to do with this company, and now I'm making sure he won't have to worry about it."

"He's still your son," said Jack.

"Goddammit!" shouted Henry, slamming a hand on the surface of the desk so hard it made Doug's pen bounce. "You stubborn son of a bitch! What's done is done, and I don't need you bringing him around trying to change my mind! Patrick's out. He wanted out and now he's out."

Patrick put a hand on Jack's arm to stop him from responding.

"What difference does it make?" asked Patrick, making no effort to lower his voice. "He's right. He's handling it like a child," he said, scowling at his father, "but he's right. I don't want anything to do with the company. He, Sean, and Bryan can divvy it up among themselves. I honestly don't care."

For a moment, Patrick thought Jack had listened to him and that they could make their retreat without further damage. But Jack, without a word to Patrick, without so much as a change in his expression, turned back to Henry.

"What have you done, Henry?" he asked softly.

"I'm not a young man. It's time," said Henry. He lowered his eyes for a fraction of a second and, in so doing, seemed to galvanize Jack's already steely mien.

"We've talked about this, Henry," said Jack. "We talked about several different plans. Different scenarios. We talked about a *process*, not a knee-jerk reaction."

Jack worked his way slowly around the table until he stood behind Doug Castin. He reached over and tapped Doug's notebook.

"What am I going to read if I open this?" he asked Henry. "What are the notes for this meeting going to say?"

"They're not going to say anything that you didn't already know," said Henry. "Not that I owe you an explanation."

"A secret meeting after everyone has gone home, and you're telling me this is what we've talked about?"

"Fine. You're going to find out soon enough anyway," said Henry. He nodded toward Bryan, who took a sheaf of papers out of a folder and slid them toward Jack.

Patrick watched closely as Jack scanned the pages. He watched Jack's furrowed brow. He watched his eyes flick from line to line. And yet his face told Patrick nothing of what the documents stated. When Jack was done, he placed the papers carefully on the table.

"Henry," said Jack, "what have you done?"

"What do you mean, 'what have I done?' I did what was necessary."

"What's it say?" asked Patrick.

"This isn't at all what we talked about," said Jack. "No contingency? No prohibition against resale of ownership? This is a live document?"

A hint of a smirk crossed Henry's face.

"Bryan?" said Henry.

Bryan opened his mouth to speak, but the man seated to his left, whom Patrick did not know, spoke over him.

"Yes sir, Mr. Kent. It's been signed and dated by all interested parties, and it's been notarized. It's an official document."

Henry nodded solemnly. Patrick noticed that Sean wore a look of smug satisfaction. Jack picked up the contract once more and flipped to the last page, then looked aghast at Henry.

"Signed and dated, indeed," said Jack. "Is this why you hid this from me? How long have you been planning this?"

"Jack?" said Patrick.

"What it says, Patty, is that your brothers are now co-owners of Coastal Seafood and all of its holdings."

"So? Dad made that announcement at the party."

"It says that Sean and Bryan here each now own forty-nine percent of the company, and your father retains two percent. What it doesn't say, however, is anything about performance requirements. It doesn't say anything about resale. This contract contains no safety measures whatsoever. It reduces your father permanently and without recourse to a minority-share owner."

Jack tossed the contract onto the table and faced Henry again. "It is not what we talked about."

"It's fine," said Henry. "It'll be fine. I maintain my two percent ownership so that neither Sean nor Bryan holds a majority. They'll have to agree on policy and, if they don't, I'll act as tiebreaker. And I'll still maintain my office here. I'll be the nominal head of the company so that our suppliers and partners don't get spooked by the transition."

"And what if *they* overrule *you*?" asked Jack. "Or what if one sells to the other? What if they both sell to a third party?"

Jack stopped, closed his eyes, and pinched the bridge of his nose using his index finger and thumb.

"Sean, Bryan," Jack said. "Please understand. I would never impugn either of you or your ability to run this company. You are its heirs. My concern here is that this takeover has not been conducted in a judicious manner. It's a very large company with a very complicated future, and I think due diligence must be done to ensure a smooth transition. We have partners, employees, vendors, suppliers—a lot of people who would be thrown off by sudden or erratic changes."

"Plus, you're worried that Bryan and I will run the company into the ground, right?" said Sean.

"No, Sean. That's not it."

"I think it is," said Sean, rising from his chair. "I think you're afraid that we'll run this company into the ground and your job will disappear. Or," Sean stopped short. He raised his eyebrows and pointed a finger at Patrick. "Or, since you and Patrick are such good buddies, you think that if he were a part-owner, your job would be secure. That's why you brought him, right? That's why you're so opposed to this arrangement. You think you can work for Pat once the old man retires, right? If he's in, you're in."

Patrick watched as Sean stood triumphant, fists resting on his hips, awash in an addled and incomplete epiphany. He looked from Sean to Jack and saw for the first time a hint of concern as the room devolved steadily toward Sean's erroneous paranoia.

"Please don't misunderstand me, Sean. This is not about me or my position here. There are much larger things at stake."

"Jack," said Sean, "if you're so worried about your job security, then let me put the matter to rest. You're fired."

A post-concussive silence filled the room. The faces at the table froze. Eyes darted anxiously from Sean to Jack and back.

"Yeah, right," said Patrick with a snicker. "Get the hell out of here, Sean. You can't fire Jack. Who the hell do you think you are?"

"Who the hell am I? Who the hell am *I*? I'll tell you who I am. I'm the majority owner of this company, Patty. That's who I am. And as such, I say that Jack Kent is removed from his duties. Effective immediately."

"You and Bryan hold equal shares. You can't have two majority owners, jackass. Wasn't that the point?"

Henry held up his hand.

"All right, that's enough," he said. "Why don't we all just calm down. Jack, you are, of course, not fired. Sean, you can't fire Jack. He's been here since the beginning. And he works for me and I say he's got a job for as long as I say he does."

"I'm afraid it's not that simple, Dad," said Sean. "According to the agreement we just made, Bryan and I can overrule you."

Patrick looked sidelong at Bryan. He was a few shades paler than he had been moments before and sweat was beginning to bead on his brow.

"Bryan, you agree with me, I assume?" said Sean with barely concealed derision.

"Well, I don't know," spluttered Bryan. "It's just that . . . well . . . it's just that . . ." he trailed off, staring wide-eyed at Sean with one hand stuck in the air, suspended palm-up as if his inert anatomy had been frozen in a living monument to his own indecision.

While the rest of the room watched in astonishment as his brother seemed paralyzed by his dilemma, Patrick watched Jack. He knew that Jack rarely found speaking of himself relevant to any discussion. He was, however, surprised to see that even with his future hanging by a thread in front of him, Jack would not speak in his own defense. He stood erect, almost at attention, with his hands clasped behind his back. His jaw was thrust out, his mouth tightly pressed closed. Only his eyes moved as he watched the spectacle unfold. He looked solid, intractable, not defiant but wholly unrepentant. He looked unmoved, unwavering, immovable.

Patrick felt a surge of loyalty for Jack. During the entire exchange, Jack's only personal concern was that his motives might be mistaken for selfish. He did not care whether he was the casualty of the idiotic crossfire in the room; he did not seem concerned how groundless or capricious his dismissal might be.

Sean grew impatient.

"Don't you agree, Bryan, that Jack poses a threat to both of us? Isn't it obvious that he's too loyal to Dad and Patrick to ever advocate for us? Don't you understand that he'll undo everything we've earned if we don't remove him from power?"

"That is preposterous!" shouted Henry. "Preposterous! And it doesn't matter anyway. He works for *me*."

"And that's fine," said Sean. "He can be your personal assistant.

He can be your chauffeur if you want. Hell, he can be your butler. But he can't work for the company and he can't set foot on any of our properties."

Patrick had seen the wrath of his father numerous times, but he had never seen him desperate. He watched as the old man's face reddened and his eyes bulged, darting frantically around the room.

"Bryan," said Henry. "Listen to me. How long have you known Jack? He's practically family. He's meant more to this company than your brother can ever comprehend. You can't let him go. You'll both need him. No one knows this place better than he does."

And in one swift moment, what Patrick had assumed would happen, did. Bryan, caught hopelessly in the crossfire between his brother and father, looked desperately to his wife. Tight-lipped and hard-faced, Helen shook her head briskly.

"You need to listen to your brother," she said. "You need to side with him."

Bryan leaned back in his chair, breathing hard. He nodded slowly, and Sean clapped his hands together.

The thing was done.

"All right then," said Sean. "It's settled. Jack, you're out. Sorry."

"Wait," said Patrick. "Wait. You can't be serious. Everyone just needs to stop and think for a second. This is ridiculous."

"Patty, I don't know how else to say it: This is none of your concern," said Sean.

"Get the hell out of here. He's got kids in college. For Christ's sake, Sean," said Patrick, but his brother was impassive.

"Patty, it's done," said Jack.

"But this is crazy," Patrick argued, turning to his father. "Dad, come on. There's got to be something you can do . . ." But Patrick stopped short. His father was staring around the room at each face in turn, leaning on the table for support, feebly mouthing his own silent disbelief.

"Patty, it's fine," said Jack. "It's time to go."

"It's not fine!" shouted Patrick. "Has everyone in this room lost their mind?"

He looked around the room. Only Sean's eyes met his. Patrick pointed a quivering finger at him. He wished his brother harm. He wished to set fire to the entire room and lock the door. But he didn't have the words. He had never had the words.

"This isn't right," was all he managed.

He turned and he left. Jack followed him. The arrogant set of his brother's jaw and the malevolence in his eyes burned so brightly in Patrick's mind that he had a hard time seeing his way down the hall.

CHAPTER NINE

He was seventeen and often in the sort of trouble typical of a seventeen-year-old boy. He was, however, aware that the reasons for his trouble were largely environmental and that his current surroundings were not good for him, which was a level of awareness not at all typical of a seventeen-year-old boy. So, when the time came, he chose a college far away on the other side of the country.

It was a small college along the Pacific coast not far from San Francisco. He chose to study marine biology because he liked the water and was pretty good with science but terrible with words. He was not a good student; it did not come easily for him. But he worked hard and was at least moderately interested in his studies, so he got by.

Outside the classroom, he did fine. He was a big kid and affable and fit reasonably well into the west coast temperament. He settled down; the trouble he had found in high school went away on its own or was displaced by other things, and some of it fell into the "normal college life" category and didn't really count as trouble after a certain age anyway. He came home during breaks and worked, and the work was hard enough in the heat of the North Carolina summer to keep him quiet. There were no more smashed-up cars or calls from the police at three in the morning.

When he returned to school for his final year, he was feeling pretty good about things in general, despite nagging thoughts about what he would do after graduation. He felt the inexorable pull of the family trade tugging at him; his father had been pleased with his choice of study and felt it was a natural fit. And Patrick, still young, had never actually considered any alternative. He had never rebelled against the idea of going into the family business because it had never occurred to him to do so, hadn't occurred to him any more than he would have thought to rebel against the notion of the sun rising. Such things existed on a plane beyond the reach of his preference.

Yet sometimes at night when he heard the ocean outside his apartment window, he felt as if his world was smaller than that of his peers. The ocean, the water, had been the constant of his young life. He had hardly spent a day away from it in some form or other, and whether three thousand miles away or right outside his window, it was the same. When he was in bed on those quiet, lonely, claustrophobic nights, the dark room with the sound of the water outside wasn't any different or any farther away than his bedroom at home and his home waters. As far as Patrick was concerned, "Atlantic" and "Pacific" were arbitrary titles. All water was the same water; if "ocean" was the agreed upon word, then all water was the ocean.

And for him, all of the ocean connected him to Spring Tide. Besides, he did not have a dream or a goal or even an alternate plan of employment. His soul had nothing that burned brightly enough to guide him away from his inevitable future. And he liked Spring Tide. He liked the people and, aside from the rusty, clanging moving parts of his family, he had enjoyed his childhood of rowing boats and digging for clams. So with nothing compelling him to leave his childhood home and in the absence of a strong enough disincentive to return to it, it seemed inevitable that he would simply allow the world's slant to roll him home.

Then one day, early in his final semester, Jack appeared on campus and took the needle off the record.

He was leaving class when he saw Jack outside the building. He noticed him only because he looked so out of place on campus, a carefully-dressed man in a dark suit standing in a world of shorts.

"It's your mother," he said without preamble.

They had known about her failing heart for some time, but she had not told her youngest son how bad it was becoming because she had not wanted to worry him. When she sensed the end drawing near, however, she sent for her son, sent Jack across the country to bring her boy home.

"The doctor says weeks, maybe days," said Jack when Patrick asked.

"Nobody called me," said Patrick.

"I think they didn't want you to find out on the phone with you out here by yourself," he said, but Patrick did not believe him and was sure they had either not cared or did not want to be bothered, but it didn't matter anyway.

The heaviness in the pit of his stomach that he had known since his mother's diagnosis suddenly became an unbearable sinking weight and he sat down because he was afraid if he didn't, it would bring him to his knees. So he sat on the steps outside the building and Jack sat quietly next to him and waited. When he was ready and felt like he could move, Jack took him back to his apartment, helped him pack, and flew him home.

The drive home reminded Patrick of the day Jack had come for him in California, and he couldn't stop reliving that trip home. Even amidst his grief and pain and fear, he had felt grateful to Jack. He was not sure how he would have made it home without him; as far as he knew, he would have sat inert on those steps forever. But mostly he had appreciated that Jack had not forced conversation during the flight home. He didn't even read or watch the in-flight movie. He just sat next to Patrick and maintained a watchful, silent vigil while Patrick sat staring out into the formless clouds with his forehead resting against the window.

Patrick sat silent once more alongside Jack as they drove through the dark. They were almost at Patrick's house before Jack broke the silence. "Bryan's weak," he said.

"Yeah," said Patrick.

When Jack didn't say anything else, Patrick glanced over at him. Jack's internal struggle was twisted onto his face. Patrick understood. He had never spoken a word against any O'Reilly family member. What had seemed to Patrick like a starkly obvious observation was for Jack a painfully trying admission.

"I've heard that when people close to the President refer to him, they find it helpful to think of the title as referring to the position and not the man, that doing so helps to mitigate any opinions one might have of the man himself. You have to separate the man from the position," said Jack, forming the words slowly as he spoke. "Patty, this is going to seem either rather ridiculous or incredibly presumptuous, but when dealing with your father, I try to maintain the same perspective. Of course, he's not exactly the President, but he is the center of a very small universe. He is jobs, he is money, he is security to thousands of people. Thinking of it in that way makes my job much easier when I have to deliver bad news or carry out an order I might not agree with," Jack said.

"Jack, you don't owe me an explanation," said Patrick.

"You know my loyalty to your family," said Jack. "But with that in mind, I'll acknowledge, now that I'm no longer employed by him, that your father can, in fact, be difficult to deal with."

Patrick hid a smile. It was amusing to him that a man was, at least in his own mind, breaking a lifetime's worth of dedication with an incredibly mild and quite obvious criticism. He felt that Jack should get his money's worth if he was going to complain.

"The man just closed an incredibly stupid deal that got you fired," said Patrick. "You can do better than 'he's a difficult person.'"

"Patty, please understand that I'm not simply airing a grievance. My point is that as much of a tyrant as he can be, as loud as he can scream, as temperamental and impatient as he might be, your father is, above all else, a very good businessman. He knows the market, he's opportunistic and aggressive, and he's competitive as hell. The same traits that make his personality so unpleasant also made him and his business extremely successful."

"Well, good for him," said Patrick.

"Again, Patty, it's not *him* I'm worried about. It's his company. His employees. When I say that this company faces a complex future, I'm not speaking in abstracts. What do you think happens when we run out of fish?"

"What do you mean, when you run out of fish? How can you run out of fish?"

"What if one day soon the earth's fish biomass is so overfished that it can't sustain itself anymore? What happens when there are no more fish?"

"Come on, Jack," said Patrick. "It's a big ocean."

"It's a finite ocean. And it's a hungry planet."

"Yeah, but is that really a pressing problem? I mean, is that really going to happen?"

"Ask the cod fishermen in Gloucester. Or the oystermen in the Chesapeake. Or look what we did to the North Sea. It's an underwater desert, raked clean by dredgers. Patty, I've got all the information I can get my hands on, and I can get my hands on a lot of information. On the one hand, I've got scientists telling me we're a generation away, that right now we are fishing out the last schools on earth. On the other hand, I've got people telling me we're fine, that there's no problem, that increasing pressure on foreign nations and improvements in sustainability yields and revised quota systems are going to save the day. I just find it highly suspicious that the latter group all tend to be employed by the same kind of person I was employed by.

"Patrick, I know you've chosen not to be a part of the company and that's your right. But I also know you care about this town and your neighbors. I suspect that, while you and your father may not see eye-to-eye on some things, you don't want to see his life's work go to ruin."

Jack had him. Patrick knew it and he suspected Jack did as well. Jack continued.

"There are very real and very specific problems that we face, and while your father thought that I was too much of an alarmist, he was at least beginning to acknowledge the possibile difficulties that lie ahead. He is, beyond all else, an old fisherman, and fishermen are all the same. They want to fish. They don't want to hear about things like ecology and environmentalist groups, but they also don't want the fish to run out. I wasn't trying to get him to give up the only industry he knows. I was just trying to get him to see the possibility of a future beyond simply pillaging the oceans, a future that involved sustainability as well as profit. I was talking about diversifying, about research and development of new ideas. I was talking about this company being a leader, an innovator in green fishing, in aquaculture. And, little by little, I was getting through. He was beginning to hear me. And then today happened. This was an absolute disaster."

"But why? Aren't the problems the same whether or not my father is in charge?" asked Patrick.

"The problems are the same. It's the solutions. The solutions won't be there. Sean is not your father," said Jack.

"Sure sounds like him most of the time," said Patrick.

"Exactly. He *sounds* like him. Sean mimics your father, but he fails to see the inner workings. He doesn't understand the situation. Sean is all bluster. He's as hostile and aggressive as your father but without any of the analysis or goal-driven business sense. He wants the title, he wants the money, he wants the status. Your father was interested in the product itself. Sean will never understand, much less care about, the theoretical underpinnings of this company's future until they become obvious, and once such things have manifested, it'll be too late. We'll be a dinosaur. And the town will die."

"That's a long way off, though, isn't it?" Patrick said.

"No one can say. But does it matter how far off it is? If you're aware of something, then it's happening now."

"But wasn't this inevitable?" asked Patrick. "The old man couldn't live forever. At some point, you had to assume Sean was going to take over."

"Sure. Of course. We had talked about an exit strategy for him, but we had talked about a gradual process that would have allowed you guys to learn what you needed to know."

"'You guys'? You mean Sean and Bryan."

"No, I mean the three of you. It was always your father's plan to leave you three the business when he had moved on. We had discussed a much slower transfer of power where he would retain majority control until such time as he felt you were fully prepared to take over. Or, of course, until he finally accepted that you didn't want to be a part of it and came up with an alternate plan. What happened tonight was rushed and pointless. Sean will steer Bryan whichever way he pleases. Your father's two-percent stake will mean nothing. It'd be different if Bryan could square up to Sean, but, well—"

"But Bryan is weak," said Patrick.

Jack nodded.

"Simply put, Bryan isn't strong enough and Sean isn't smart enough to run this company," said Jack.

Patrick was startled by the bluntness of the words. He leaned back in his seat and watched the lights of the town pass by as they navigated the silent Main Street of Spring Tide that ran perpendicular to the waterfront.

"Jack, did I cost you your job tonight?" Patrick asked.

"No," said Jack firmly, immediately.

"It seems like this is all happening because of me. It seems like my father just gave away his entire life's work, and inadvertently cut you out of his own company just to spite me. If I had humored him a little, maybe none of this would have happened."

Jack puffed out his cheeks, then expelled a breath slowly and loudly.

"You did nothing wrong, Patrick, and you shouldn't have to humor him. Certainly not on my behalf. I would never put you in a position where you had to be untrue to yourself. There was nothing either of us could have done tonight that would have helped. And it isn't your job to make sure I have a job."

They turned into Patrick's driveway but he did not get out of the car.

"So what now?" he asked.

"I honestly don't know," said Jack. "But you need to be careful. Don't do anything rash."

"What are you going to do?"

"I'll be fine. Don't worry about me."

"Jack, for what it's worth, if I had known this would happen, I would have joined the company a long time ago."

"Patty, I know you would have. And I appreciate that. You're a good man. But it would have been the biggest mistake of your life."

Jack backed out of the driveway and, in the stillness of the night, the sound of the car driving away lingered. Patrick stood in the driveway for a long time as the warm, dank smell of the marsh drifted from the reedy banks behind his house, the smell that more than anything else marked that one small spot in the world as his home.

CHAPTER TEN

All things bend to hard work.

He had heard the saying somewhere a long time ago and thought it trite at the time but it had stuck with him long enough to prove true, at least as true as anything else. He had trained his mind to the work like a distance runner trains his lungs to carry him, and the saying made him feel as if there perhaps was more to the work he did than just the structures he built.

He applied the words like a salve, like a religion. It became his solution to a world that asked him to think about it far more often and in far more depth than he cared to. It was a wall; a simple, sturdy wall, and he placed himself on one side alongside his crew and his boat and his tools and kept all other things on the other side of it.

For a few days it worked. Jack's firing kept him awake most of the night and it still burned hot all the next day. But the aphorism was stronger than the incident and it, too, bent to the hard work.

The three men completed the Porter dock. Once finished, it was as ornate as something made of wood and buried in mud could be. Two boat slips constructed of three floating docks; a wide, flat deck on one side with built-in seats; a gazebo at the end. Patrick had driven himself beyond exhaustion. He had worn out his crew, who had had to repeatedly do something they loathed and ask Patrick to call it a day once the sun had gone down and the workday had pushed into its twelfth hour.

When he drove himself to the limit of endurance, when he almost fell asleep on the ride home, when he sat down to rest for just a moment and woke up hours later still sitting upright on the couch, he didn't stay awake thinking about the quiet maelstrom that surrounded him. He worked. He slept. He did everything but talk about it.

It had not even occurred to him that he wanted to talk about it until he came home one evening and spotted Davis' car in the driveway.

"What the hell kind of hours are you working?" said Davis when Patrick pushed open the door.

"Yeah, we've been wrapping up a job," said Patrick.

"I've been hanging out with the dog for the past three hours," he said. "We've nothing left to talk about. I'll say this, though—the dog has some pretty resentful feelings towards the cat."

"Hard to blame him. That cat's got it pretty easy."

"It's not a bad life, I suppose," said Davis.

"Not a bad life? Throw in a two-hour workday and it's *your* life," said Patrick.

"Hey, the halls of academia are open to you salt-of-the-earth types too, pal."

"Oh, yeah? Plenty of openings for a permanent graduate student?"

"You bet," said Davis with a grin. "The pay leaves much to be desired. But the benefits are great."

"I don't think sleeping with your students is an official component of the school's benefit packages."

"Ah! No sir! That's where you're wrong," said Davis, wagging a finger at Patrick. "None of them are *my* students. Not current students, anyway. And I'm just a graduate assistant. It's only creepy if a *professor* sleeps with his students."

"Sure. Keep telling yourself that."

"Not without first having a very frank and open conversation with Javier and José."

Patrick grinned.

"Well, there's always a job available doing honest work if you'd ever like to get back into that sort of thing."

"Hell, no," said Davis. "Only a crazy person would be out there in the sun crawling about in the muck all day. Besides, I've already tried it. It didn't take, remember?"

"What I remember is someone bitching and moaning for about a day and a half and then quitting in a big huff."

"It was a full two weeks if it was a day! And it was long enough to know that that's the work of field animals. You and that crazy man Watts. Neither of you ever even took a break. High school kids are supposed to work at ice cream shops or lifeguard at pools or babysit or whatever. They are absolutely not supposed to haul creosote-covered logs the size of telephone poles around in the mud all day. I swear my whole world smelled like those godforsaken pilings for a month."

Patrick laughed. During the summer after they'd graduated from high school, Davis' brief stint working for Old Man Watts had consisted primarily of the obscenities that he had strewn about the marshes of Spring Tide as he dragged himself back and forth through the mud. Once he'd had enough, Davis threw down his gloves and marched off without another word. Watts just smiled as his already-solid tally of broken high school kids increased by one. His was the unyielding emotionless math of narrow profit margins and rapidly changing seasons. The impassiveness of Watts was also precisely the neutral ground upon which Patrick had sought to prove himself. Neither money nor name held any influence on the manner in which Watts plied his trade. The work was the only measure and Patrick had proven himself to his boss.

"Speaking of all things Spring Tide," said Davis, "what's this I read in the papers about your father stepping down?"

"I don't think that's what he meant to do. But that's what happened all right," said Patrick. "Then they fired Jack."

"Your father fired Jack Kent? That doesn't make any sense."

"No, Sean did. Said Jack was too close to me, and he had some idiot idea that Jack would undermine him somehow. I don't know."

"How on earth would Sean ever be in a position to fire anybody, much less Jack Kent?"

Patrick told him the whole story and when he was done, he slumped back on the couch. He felt better, lighter, but he also felt as if that meeting was alive in a way that it hadn't been before, as if the words had brought it out of its innocuous two-dimensional place in his memory and breathed life into it. He felt once again the familiar sense of some large ill-defined abstraction sliding quietly away, moving like an animal moves through the woods at night, moving out of reach before he could lay hands on it.

"Well, that's certainly a lot of palace intrigue for one night," said Davis. "What's Jack going to do now?"

Patrick shrugged.

"It'll be weird, if it stands," said Davis. "He's a legend in this town. I mean, he's an absolute hard-ass, and I bet he's the face of death if you're stealing from his boss, but his presence around town means that things are going fine down at headquarters. That kind of stability is a rarity these days. It's a luxury. I guess that's all over now."

"I hadn't really thought about it like that," said Patrick. "I just felt bad because he lost his job and it was probably because of me."

"Oh, it was definitely because of you," said Davis. "But it wasn't your fault."

"Well, there's something going on here. Something's not right."

"It does seem a bit strange that your dad would retire with so little warning. And without Jack being in the loop, at that," said Davis.

"It's more than that, though. I can't put my finger on it. I know there's something else, something I'm not seeing."

"You're not as familiar with the business. You don't know the day-to-day well enough to be able to spot aberrations," said Davis.

"I don't know. I guess. It still seems to me that there's an answer in front of me and I'm just not seeing it."

"Refresh my memory," said Davis. "Who was at the meeting when you got there?"

"Dad, Sean, and Bryan. Bryan's wife. That kid Doug Castin. Some lawyers."

"Bryan's wife but not Sean's? That's odd, no?"

Patrick shrugged.

"Not really. They're so different. I can't imagine Suzanne being at all interested in the business. And you know what a pain in the ass Helen is," said Patrick.

"Was your dad's fiancée there?"

"Oh, right. Yeah, she was there. She doesn't really say much."

"You know about her, right?" said Davis.

"I don't know anything about her."

"Well you need to get out more." He rubbed his hands together and leaned forward. "I don't have all the details, and I'm sure I don't know all the stories, but it's pretty well-known that Marie is one of the greatest gold-diggers of all time. She's a legend among the Wilmington elites. She's been married at least a half-dozen times. She'd be nicknamed the 'Black Widow' if it wasn't so trite."

"Wait," said Patrick. "Does she kill her husbands? Is that the rumor?"

"No, it's not quite that sinister. It's more along the lines of someone who gets their horse shot out from under him. There's no real intent there or anything, but you've got to figure that you probably wouldn't want to be the next horse."

"What?" asked Patrick.

Davis waved him off.

"Put it this way: Anybody can hit one big score. Any hot young thing can find some old bastard, rub her tits on him, and make off with his estate once he kicks off. But do you know how hard it must be to get some old man to marry you *after* you've been through one already? After the 87-year-old 'love of your life' dies? Rich people are paranoid. It's not easy to sneak up on them. So how, I ask you, has Marie pulled off the trick so many times? How does she keep getting rich old men to fall for her, knowing the fates of those who've gone before them?"

"What fate? Have they all died?"

"Well, no," said Davis, slightly deflated. "Only her first husband died. I think that mostly she just gets divorced a lot. And I might have overshot by a couple with the half-dozen figure. But a nice round half-dozen makes for better storytelling, no?"

"Davis, what are the odds that most of this is urban legend?"

"I'd say the odds would be incredibly high that it is entirely urban legend, except for one thing." He held a finger in the air. "You know one of her ex-husbands."

"Yeah, right. Who?"

"Francis McLean, that's who."

"Who is Francis McLean?"

"That's certainly not the response I was looking for," said Davis. "Francis McLean? The accountant? Has a weekend house on the island? You did some work for him a couple years ago?"

"Oh, right. But he was just a client. It's not like we were friends. He's not that rich, is he? I doubt he'd be much of a target for a gold-digger."

"He's old money. Well, not so much anymore."

Patrick tried to remember the man. The face wasn't clear but he recalled that he wore glasses. He was a small man, slight of build, balding. Genial, unobtrusive, harmless. Patrick felt sorry for him.

"So I knew him. Sort of. What does that prove?"

"It proves that it's not just a myth! It proves that real people were involved, with real histories. It proves that . . . all right, I've got nothing here. The fact that one of them was a client of yours proves nothing. All the same, Marie marries people for money, and now she's engaged to your father."

"I don't know. Seems a little far-fetched. How do we know she's not just some lonely woman looking to spend the rest of her days being a little less lonely?"

"What kind of theory is that? There's no subterfuge, no Machiavellian scheming, no betrayal. There's not even an antagonist. It's ridiculous," said Davis.

"Is this what you do? Sit around and come up with paranoid fantasies, just to bother those of us with actual jobs?"

"I am being very serious."

"You are not, but I'll humor you," said Patrick. "Suppose Marie marries a man who dies, mysteriously or otherwise, and leaves her his riches. Then she marries several other men, including this poor bastard McLean, and she cleans all of them out as well. That means she's rich, right? She's already rich enough. Why would she keep at it?"

"See, you know nothing of the world, Patrick, and I know everything. Have you ever heard a rich person say, 'That's okay. I'm rich enough already'? Rich folks become rich folks by pursuing money beyond all else. They have a ruthless, single-minded focus. It's hardwired. They don't know how to stop building wealth. No rich person says 'no' to being richer. Well, except you."

"I'm not rich," said Patrick. "Check my bank account."

"You've chosen not to be rich. That's the same as being rich. You'd never do it, but the fact is you could make a single call and be back on the family chuck wagon. Like it or not, the fact that you have that choice available to you puts you in a category well beyond the reach of most people."

"Can we get back to the issue at hand? It hardly seems like Marie is the con artist you've made her out to be."

"And what, pray tell, would a con artist look like? Should she be wearing a black cap and mask and carrying a big sack with a dollar sign printed on it? Maybe she should wear a top hat and a curly mustache?

Patrick, if everyone who was out to take people's money *looked* like they were out to take people's money, no one would ever get their money taken."

"Well, maybe that's her past," said Patrick.

"Past, present, and future."

"No, I mean maybe when she was younger, she was this femme fatale that you're convinced she is, but now she's changed her ways."

"Or maybe your dad is her last big score. Maybe he's the once-in-a-lifetime score, the one that's too big to pass up. Maybe your dad is a prize that a gold-digger can only dream of and she's finally found an opening after years of keeping her eyes peeled for just such an opportunity."

"Hardly," said Patrick. "You're talking about a guy who tried to get his son to make his girlfriend sign a pre-nup. His *high school* girlfriend. I can't imagine my father leaving himself open like that."

As soon as he said it, a wave of doubt landed heavily in his midsection.

"Although," he added, "not much has made sense lately. A few weeks ago, I'd have sworn there was no way anyone could take advantage of him. But you should have seen him at that meeting. By the end of it, he looked . . . I don't know. I don't have the words."

"Defeated, perhaps?"

"Yeah, maybe."

"And that's not a guy who has a lot of losses on his record," said Davis.

"It was just so strange to see him like that. Like I said, I'm just not smart enough."

"You want a drink or something?" asked Davis.

"Sorry," said Patrick. "I should have offered."

Davis went into the kitchen and rummaged through a few cabinets. Patrick heard a bottle set heavily on a countertop and ice clink into glasses.

"You'd be able to figure this out," said Patrick over his shoulder.

"What?"

"If it was you. If you were in this situation, you'd be able to make sense of all this."

Davis came back and handed Patrick his drink.

"You're not dumb," said Davis. "You're just out of your element. You've been avoiding office politics and, well, your whole family for so long that you've lost the vocabulary for it. You don't know what you're looking at when you see it."

"Yeah, but you'd still be able to put it together."

Davis balanced his drink on the palm of his hand and spoke to the glass. "Even if that's true, I was never involved with the company. But you know who did have both the access and the intelligence?"

"Who?"

"Jack Kent," said Davis.

Patrick looked up at Davis, who looked up from his drink, raised his eyebrows, and shrugged.

"Are you saying what I think you're saying?"

"It's possible, no?" said Davis.

"Anything's possible, but you're suggesting that Sean staged some elaborate scheme to get rid of Jack so that he wouldn't be in a position to ruin things for Sean. I just don't think he has that kind of patience and foresight."

"Yeah, maybe not. He would have had to be thinking several steps ahead. It's vastly more likely that he swung blindly in a childish rage and managed to strike down the only person who's a real threat to him."

"Could be a little of both," said Patrick. "Could be that Sean just didn't like Jack because Jack is smarter than he is, or closer to Dad, or more respected. Maybe the reasons that made him so mad at Jack were the same reasons that Jack would have been able to stop him from doing whatever he's doing. Had to be a lucky accident on Sean's part. I can't imagine him as any sort of mastermind."

"It is a bit of a reach," agreed Davis. "No offense."

"If you're going to offend me by talking about Sean, you've got your work cut out for you. It's a shame, though," said Patrick. "The smartest of the three of us was probably Bryan. And now he's an empty suit."

"Bryan's definitely the weaker of the two partners," said Davis.

Patrick sat upright in his chair, a little of his drink sloshing out of the glass.

"Say that again," said Patrick.

"I said that Bryan's weak. Weaker than Sean."

Bryan's weak.

Davis cocked his head in a silent question, but Patrick was following a thread in his mind and he was afraid that if he spoke it would unravel.

Bryan's weak.

Patrick saw how it would all come undone and he was embarrassed that it had taken him so long because it seemed so incredibly obvious. It was laid out in front of him; he saw it the way he imagined chess players might see the game in their mind.

They would all take what they wanted but there was not enough of his father to go around and still keep him whole. Sean would take the company and, thus, the power. Marie would take the money, regardless of whether or not her intent was sinister. Helen wanted the status and she would have it, and it would make no difference to her that her husband was an impotent puppet. Even Bryan would get what he wanted, which was to never be asked to have an opinion. Helen would see to that.

Patrick shivered. He realized that he, too, was no innocent. He also would get what he wanted: he would be left alone. He had never considered that holding one's ground was an action and not merely the absence of motion, that to refuse to choose was itself a choice.

"An absolute disaster," Jack had called it. Patrick had never considered the components in the context of the larger situation. He had never been aware of the ramifications of his father's ruin.

His father was the town. That was the key to the whole thing. It was exactly what Jack had tried to tell him. The company, his father, the town; all three were part of the other and could not be extricated from one another. And he, too, was part of the whole; the town was his home and always had been. It was the center of his map.

It occurred to him that the town was the only thing he loved.

"The town can't survive without him, not like this," said Patrick.

"No," said Davis. "It can't."

"Everyone will take what they can, everyone will act selfishly, and my father doesn't have enough to give."

"Enough of what? Money?"

"No, it's not money," said Patrick. "Well, it is and it isn't. I'm talking about the man himself. He doesn't have enough of *himself* to give to all the people who would take from him. I'm talking about money, power, stature, stability, all of it. All of the . . . damn. All of the things Jack has been trying to tell me my whole life."

Patrick unwound the tangled thoughts for Davis, the whole complex mess of Sean and Bryan, their wives, Marie; each person's desires combined with his father's erratic behavior, made for a combustible mix, and Jack's firing was a spark.

"But here's what I don't understand," said Davis when Patrick had finished. "Not to be crass, but your father has to die sometime. This anarchy, this chaos you predict—wasn't it all inevitable?"

"That's just it," said Patrick. "That's the thing my father must have understood. He should have been planning this for years. He should have been grooming someone to take over when he was gone. They should have been preparing the employees, the town itself, to ensure some continuity, at least from a business perspective. I just don't understand. He'd never make a mistake like this. He'd never make such a rash and incredibly stupid decision with his company. And I've never seen him do anything without Jack in the loop."

"All of which begs the question," said Davis. "What are you going to do about it?"

"Well, I've got to get Jack in there somehow. He's the only voice of reason."

"Even if that were possible, and I don't think it is, would he want to go back? His loyalty was not exactly paid back with interest."

"He'd come back," said Patrick.

"How do you know?"

"Because this is bigger than my family or the company and, until a few minutes ago, he was the only person who seemed to realize it."

"But he's out. Sean made sure of it."

"I'll just have to convince Bryan to reverse it," said Patrick.

"You're going to ask Bryan to defy Sean? There's no way he'll do it, even if he does agree with you."

"He's going to have to," said Patrick. "There's no other way."

CHAPTER ELEVEN

Patrick awoke, pulled open the shades, and looked out at the water and the dull gray sky. He watched the sluggish drift of the tide, barely evident in the mirror-flat waterway. He noted the stillness of the marsh grasses in the still-lifeless dawn. He could tell that the day would be breezy, even though it was calm at the moment, and that there would be no rain.

He liked the early gray hour after the sun broke free of the ocean, before its rays peeked above the row of houses on the island. It was the only time of the day when there were no boats on the waterway except for the occasional trawler heading out to sea. It was the time before the wind rose and chopped up the water's surface, before the marsh birds resumed their never-ending Sisyphean fishing and gathering, before there were any bright colors or sharp angles, before humanity made itself boisterously and obtrusively known. Soon, he would drive stakes into the place where water meets land, build on top of it, and he would do it without remorse. But he liked the soft, quiet, solitary hour and the flat water, the great unflexed muscle of the marsh as it lay docile and nonthreatening. He was at peace with the water around him and at least at a détente with the rest of the world.

He would go see Bryan, but he had work to do first. He had to motor the barge down to Mr. Macready's place, then take delivery of the large posts that would become pilings. But he would go in the afternoon as soon as he could get away. He had tossed and turned all night and had only fallen asleep after deciding not to put it off. Nonetheless, as he stood at the window, he thought only fleetingly about the impending conversation. With at least the illusion, at that early hour, that all who might trouble him still slumbered, outside circumstances never intruded upon his morning reverie.

He made no plans, he did no math, he pondered no questions. He stood peacefully without thought until he was ready to go and that moment at the slim edge between the previous day and the beginning of the new one was his only ritual that was not work.

When not in use, the barge remained tied off at the end of his dock. It was not a fancy craft; it was barely seaworthy. He had inherited it from his previous boss, who had built it himself, and Patrick had never been sure to what extent Watts had intended it to be anything more than a temporary solution to a permanent problem; namely, the lack of a solid, stable platform in a liquid world.

The barge was nothing more than a flat, twenty-foot square of metal that somehow managed to float. It had a flying bridge from which Patrick could steer and look out over the bow, twin diesel engines for propulsion and maneuvering, a large generator and pump, and a crane forward of the bridge used to pick up the pilings and hold them in place.

When Javier and José arrived groggy-eyed at five minutes to eight, the three men boarded the barge together. Patrick brought the engines up to temperature while the men cleared the deck of any loose objects and tied lines to the crane to secure it while underway. They tethered Patrick's johnboat to the stern, untied the dock lines, and eased into the waterway.

The Macready house sat on a small creek that branched off the waterway a few miles south of Patrick's house and opened into a flat backwater that formed an aquatic cul-de-sac. A handful of single-story bungalows sat clustered around the creek. Patrick steered toward a small, green house with a huge, Spanish moss-covered oak in the backyard whose long limbs stretched comfortably outward like a cat after a nap. They had arrived during a slack tide and the anchoring went smoothly. They set three anchors in order to minimize the barge's drift until they had time to bury the first piling and tie one corner to it to give the vessel some permanent footing.

A dock shapes the land over which it sits. It affects how water flows around it, dictating where sand or mud gathers or washes away, which in turn determines where and what type of grasses and reeds grow, which affects what sort of animals prey and are preyed upon in the vicinity. It may take months, it may take years, it may take only a single powerful storm. But a dock inevitably changes the surroundings upon which it rests.

Well aware of the active role that a passive collection of wood can play, Patrick had chosen the location of the pilings with great care. It took him and his crew several days to align and measure the locations, but there was no step more important than that first step. He had picked a spot on the property far enough from the neighbors' docks so as not to interrupt the flow of water and long enough to ensure deep water for Mr. Macready's boat, but not so long that the neighbors would be upset by a dock jutting too far out into the creek. When he was satisfied, they drove orange stakes into the ground to mark the spots. Then they waited for a calm day.

Once the barge was anchored and secured and the old, rusty workhorse prepped for yet another job, they waited for the truck to deliver the wood. Patrick and his men were uncomfortable waiting. Their relationship was built on motion, and they could communicate well while working but could carry on only the most cursory of conversations when idle. They were also not acclimated to lazing about, and none of the three knew what to do with his hands. José and

Javier sat on the barge slightly apart from Patrick, who busied himself recoiling a twice-coiled line, and all three periodically looked up the road toward the front of the house.

When the flatbed finally lumbered into the driveway, Patrick's men helped as much as they could to roll the massive posts off the truck and down the backyard's slight slope to the edge of the water. The wood was of varying sizes. The smaller posts were used closer to land, while the biggest pilings, wider than a man and weighing almost as much as a small car, were used to anchor the farthest edge of the dock in the deeper water.

After the unloading, Patrick toyed with the idea of getting started right away, but the tide had come in while they were waiting and it was too deep to work. Reluctantly, he untied his boat from the barge and motored back up the waterway to his dock. He let Javier and José go for the day, then went inside, showered, and put on clean clothes.

He stopped at the edge of his driveway before turning onto the road. He was wracked by doubt, but that he had expected. He was far out of his element, unsure of what he was going to say, and not at all sure it would make a difference. What he found disconcerting was his complete lack of instinct. There was nothing, not a sound from within. He'd have been comfortable proceeding into a dangerous situation or one unlikely to end successfully if he was at least firm in his conviction. He was also fine with giving up, if that's where his conscience led him. But without so much as a guess at what the right thing to do might be, he was lost.

When he arrived at the house, a maid let him in to wait in the foyer, and as he looked around, he remembered that Bryan's house was not, in fact, Bryan's house in any real way. It was a nice house; it was a large, new-looking house in a new-looking neighborhood with new-looking roads and lawns and cars in the driveways. The inside was suspiciously clean for a house that was home to a four-year-old. The furniture was severe and uninviting, the windows draped in several layers of silk, and the walls decorated with blurry paintings that Patrick didn't understand and whose primary function seemed to be pretentiousness. Nothing about the house, inside or out, resembled Bryan in any way. He had a room in the basement where he was allowed to keep his stuff. The rest of the house was Helen's.

"Oh, hey Patty," said Bryan without surprise, as if Patrick appearing unannounced in his foyer was commonplace. "I figured you'd come by."

"You did? Why?"

"Because we fired Jack and you'd come here to try to talk me out of it."

"Really?"

"You sound surprised."

"I don't mean to be rude, but I didn't think you were . . ."

Patrick trailed off. He could not think of a nice way to finish the sentence. He supplied the rest of the thought with a shrug.

"Oh, I know," said Bryan. "Everybody assumes I'm asleep at the wheel. And now here you are, about to ask me to overrule Sean, to bring Jack back and restore Dad to his rightful place at the head of the table and all of that."

Patrick stood flabbergasted. He wondered if Bryan had been working some incredibly masterful angle, if he had been playing the fool for years and was now set to spring a trap on a shocked world.

"I don't understand," said Patrick. "If you knew all of that, why didn't you just do something?"

"When?"

"Hell, I don't know. When it happened, I guess. Look, Bryan, help me out here. I thought I was going to have to make some sort of fiery speech which, to tell the truth, I was dreading. You've caught me off guard here."

"Yeah, no problem," said Bryan. "Come in, take a load off."

Patrick followed Bryan into the den. He took a seat on a small sofa whose back was so upright it felt as if it was past vertical. Bryan slumped into a leather chair across from him.

"Patty, there's a big difference between not knowing what's going on and not caring about what's going on."

"So you don't care about any of this? You don't care about the company that's now part yours?"

"Oh, I care that the money keeps rolling in. But as far as which direction we take, no, I don't really care. And I'm sorry about Jack. I really am. But Sean wanted him gone, so he's gone. End of story."

"What do you mean, 'end of story'? You don't care that you're Sean's puppet? You don't care that everyone sees his arm sticking out of your ass?"

"You got yourself a pretty nice view from the cheap seats, eh?" said Bryan. Anger flashed in his eyes but flared out just as fast. "Look, Patty, you've got your own thing going there with your construction gig, and I think that's great. Good for you. Hell, I admire you for doing it. There's no future in it, of course, but at least you're out there doing what you want to do. Point is, I don't bother you about your business, do I?"

"Yes, you do," said Patrick.

"Well, maybe a suggestion here or there," said Bryan, "but by and large, I don't come poking around in your affairs, judging every move, second-guessing every decision you make, do I?"

"Bryan, I'm not trying to butt in where I don't belong. There are bigger things at play here. This company is more than—"

"Oh, blah, blah, blah," interrupted Bryan, rolling his eyes. "If I wanted to hear that God-and-country, 'this company is the heart and soul of the community' bullshit, I'd go ask Dad for his thoughts. Hell, I'm glad he won't be around all the time. Who needs to hear his constant bellowing? He doesn't even make sense half the time."

"Well, surely you can agree that, if nothing else, there's a good chance the money will dry up, right?"

"How do you figure?"

"For starters, suppose you and Sean run the damn business into the ground."

"Won't happen. Even if Sean is completely incompetent, which could definitely be the case, the strongest likelihood is that we'd just sell to someone. Or go public and be run by a board of directors. Either way, they'd have to pay me my half for the privilege."

"All right. What if the fish run out?"

"Don't get me started on Jack's scare tactics. It's alarmist nonsense. We're not going to run out of fish. Actually," he hesitated. "We'll pretty much definitely run out of fish, but it won't be in my lifetime. So what difference does it make?"

"Jesus, Bryan, you should be a motivational speaker," said Patrick.

"Patty, you have to understand that Sean is going to win one way or another. That's how it's always been. If I go along with him, my life's easy. If I challenge him, I bring a bunch of shit on myself that I have to slog through and I still don't win. I learned a long time ago that the best bet is to just go along with it. I've got a pretty decent thing going here. So if you want to get Sean to change his mind, go talk to him yourself."

Patrick looked carefully at Bryan. Bryan looked away. Once Patrick had sized him up, he stood.

"That is, without a doubt, the biggest load of bullshit I have ever heard in my life," said Patrick. "You're telling me that you can't do the right thing for a family friend because your big brother is mean to you? You're a grown man! What the hell's the matter with you?"

"Come on, Patty," said Bryan. "Do you really think it matters? Do you really think it makes a difference? If it's not Sean, it's Dad. If it's not Dad, it's . . . the other. Don't you join the list."

"Who's 'the other'?"

"You know," said Bryan, and he flicked his eyes sharply upwards twice, in the direction of the upstairs.

"Helen?"

"Would you keep your voice down?" hissed Bryan.

Patrick snorted and shook his head.

"You have got to be kidding me," he said. "Why on earth did you marry her if you're so afraid of her?"

"That's none of your business."

"Is it because they told you to? Because Dad or Sean told you to marry her? Or did Helen tell you to? It sure as hell couldn't have been your idea. You don't have ideas."

"Go to hell, Patty. You don't know what you're talking about."

"I don't know what I'm talking about? I'll tell you what I do know. I know you're too afraid of your own wife to get Jack his job back and make this thing right. I know you're too afraid of your own family to do the right thing."

"Your brother has no reason to be afraid of me," came Helen's voice from the top of the stairs. Patrick heard her heels clicking downward before he saw her. She came to a stop in the doorway to the living room and folded her arms across her chest. "He knows that if he ever defied me, I'd leave him. So there's no reason for him to be afraid. We understand each other perfectly well."

Bryan stood, hands in pockets, drooped like a withered plant, looking very much like a man trying to either become part of the floor or disappear through it. He looked at neither Patrick nor Helen. He said nothing.

"If he *defies* you? Who do you think you are?" asked Patrick.

"I'm his wife, that's who I am. And as such, I'm entitled to half of everything he owns. Which now includes half of the Coastal Seafood holdings."

"The weaker half."

Helen thrust her jaw in the air and took a step in Patrick's direction.

"Bryan may not be the most, shall we say, aggressive businessman in the world, but that's why he has me. I offer him the counsel he needs to manage the business. We're a team."

"Does he get to sleep inside or do you have a little house for him out back?"

Helen thrust a finger in Patrick's direction but caught herself and smiled. "I pity you, Patrick. All you have are your snide jokes. You could've been handed all of this." She made a sweeping gesture around the house. "But you gave it up. It's a shame, really."

"You're aware that this whole act of yours was bought and paid for by my family, right? You know that, don't you? I'm not sure who you're trying to impress. Bryan and I have the same father. It's the same family you're trying to fleece."

Helen maintained her composure, but just barely. Her cheeks glowed red and her eyes bulged.

"OK, Patty, let's take it easy," said Bryan, his voice so small that Patrick thought for a moment it was coming from another room.

Bryan was holding both his hands out as if to prevent his brother and wife from physically attacking each other. But he was standing far enough away from both of them that his hands did nothing beyond form a useless obtuse triangle.

"Is there any point to your life, Bryan?" asked Patrick. The harshness of the question escaped without his consent. But he could not stop. "Is there anything left of you at all? You don't give a damn about anything that matters. You're married to this horrible thing over here," he said, jerking a thumb in Helen's direction. "What is it you're doing? Why do you live this way?"

"Are you going to stand there and let him speak to me like that in my own home?" asked Helen.

"Wait. *Now* you want him to jump in? After he stood here like a stump and watched this whole conversation? *Now* you feel like he needs to jump in and defend your honor?"

Helen ignored him.

"Bryan, you need to tell your brother to leave. You need to tell him that he is no longer welcome in this house."

"Why do you take this? I need to know, Bryan. Why do you choose this life?" asked Patrick.

"You are such an idiot," said Helen, shaking her head in derision. "Don't you get it? If we got divorced, I would get half of his share of the company. Twenty-four and a half percent, to be precise."

"For the love of God, Bryan, who gives a shit? Aren't there enough millions in just a quarter of the damn company?"

"Tell him, Bryan," said Helen. "Go ahead."

Bryan looked pleadingly at Helen. His mouth hung open in a protest that died on the vine. He looked back toward Patrick's feet.

"Dad would never tolerate an outsider holding a percentage in the company," he said, his voice, his entire affect, flat. "I can't get divorced. She can't have a percentage of the company."

"What about the pre-nup?"

"We . . . well, we didn't . . . we decided not to sign a pre-nup," said Bryan.

Out of the corner of his eye, Patrick saw Helen smile.

"Let me guess. You told Dad you'd signed one to make him happy," said Patrick.

Bryan nodded again.

"Does Sean know?"

Once more, Bryan nodded again.

"So he can put the screws to you whenever he wants."

Patrick looked at his brother and felt pity. He was angry at the sensation.

"All of this mess, just so that your father won't be mad at you. Or ashamed of you, or whatever your problem is. Believe me, I don't want to know. Wait. How did Sean find out?"

"Bryan," interjected Helen. "You need to make him leave."

"You didn't tell him, did you?" asked Patrick.

"Right now!" Helen said, her voice nearly a shriek. "You need to tell him to leave right now! He is no longer welcome in my house!"

"*You* should leave, Bryan," said Patrick. "What's the worst that could happen? Dad would be disappointed in you. So what? Believe me, you'd survive that."

"This is your last warning," said Helen, and Patrick wasn't sure whom she was addressing.

"*She* told Sean, Bryan. She told him!" Patrick said.

"You tell him to leave!" Helen screamed. "You tell him right now! *Right now* or I will walk out that door!"

"Come on, Bryan. She went behind your back and told Sean about the pre-nup thing. Just to trap you. You don't have to live like this."

Bryan's morose gaze flickered between Helen and Patrick. Something large and heavy hung in the room and pressed down on Bryan. Patrick could feel the fight in him, could feel a glimmer of a long-forgotten primordial hope somewhere inside his brother. But Helen changed her attack. She put one hand on her husband's arm and the other under his chin, turned his face toward hers, more gently than Patrick imagined possible. Her face was calm and smooth, the fight carried only in her eyes as she forced Bryan to look into them.

"You need to listen to me, Bryan," she said. "This is important. This is one of those times when you need to trust me."

It was all she said. Whatever hope or malevolence, past or future, promise or threat that she carried in the words and in the manner in which she delivered them remained unspoken. But something in Bryan broke under the strain and Patrick saw the fight in him die and knew it was done before Bryan spoke.

"Patty, you need to leave," he said. He did not look at Patrick.

"And?" added Helen, one hand still on his arm.

Bryan mumbled something inaudible.

"What was that?" asked Patrick.

"And you're no longer welcome in our home," said Bryan, only slightly louder.

"Well, I never really was, was I?" said Patrick but he did not wait for a response.

Helen moved to hold the door open and, radiating smugness, watched Patrick leave. The door slammed behind him, the knocker clattering against itself.

He threw the Jeep in reverse and sped out of the driveway. The tires squealed in protest as he flew onto the road. He drove until his breathing calmed, circled through the wide roads and around the gentle curves of the neighborhood until his nostrils stopped flaring and his grip loosened on the wheel.

There are no secrets in fishing towns. He knew that Marie and Bryan lived in the same neighborhood, that he was already close to her house. He drove past it once, pretending it was by accident, then looped around again and came to a stop out front and stared at the wide brick façade and immense pillars.

What Davis had said about her, however farfetched or unfair it might have been, had stayed with him. And while he could manufacture no legitimate reason to see if she was home beyond his own curiosity, and perhaps the desire to get the bitter taste of his failure with Bryan out of his mouth, the unshaped idea that she might have some insight about his father tantalized him. He set aside the unease of being somewhere he did not belong and approached the house.

He knocked on the door and was not surprised when a young maid answered. A wordless but not impolite wave of a hand ushered him in and directed him into a room off the foyer. A sudden rush of silence gripped the place. He turned but the maid was gone, vanished into the spotless wasteland of the house. He assumed she had gone to announce his presence to Marie, but the house seemed too impossibly ordered and clean to have ever hosted a human life. Patrick was lost, adrift in a place where ordinary codes of interaction may not apply and the maid may have gone anywhere, may have been anyone gone to do anything. His childhood had been spent in wealth, certainly, but his mother had always valued their home as more than a physical space and had gone to great lengths to make sure it felt as lived-in as it was.

He lifted a foot self-consciously to make sure his boots had not left a mark on the white carpet of the room; the room was adorned with only carpet, drapes, and two couches facing one another, both unerringly white. It was a smudgeless room, a room that had hosted neither spilled drinks nor children's unwashed hands nor any human mistake whatsoever, or if it had done so, it held them close as a secret.

A clicking in the hall grew louder, footsteps spaced in a hurried cadence, and Patrick felt relieved at the promise of escaping the room, though that relief was tempered by a hollow sound somewhere in his chest.

Marie sped into the entryway, then stopped abruptly, no more than a foot inside the room. She looked Patrick over once, quickly, and cocked her head. She crossed her arms over her chest and offered a smile that was cordial but no more welcoming than the angle of her folded arms.

"Yes?" she said.

Patrick stalled, not certain why he was there or what he had come to accomplish. And the sinking sensation that she didn't have any idea who he was didn't help to clarify the situation.

"Hey," he said. "Hi."

She blinked once. "May I help you?"

"I wondered if we might . . . we don't know each other very well," he said.

She blinked again. The stretched-tight skin on her face seemed to tighten a bit more but her head did not move.

"It's me," he said. He felt the blood rise in his cheeks. "Patrick. Patrick O'Reilly."

Her eyebrows shot upward, her hands went up and backward and she bent slightly backward at the waist. "Patrick! Of course! So good to see you again. So sorry. For a moment, I thought you were one of the contractors. It's been just a zoo here lately with everything that's going on." She gestured toward the rest of the house.

Patrick heard no sounds whatsoever either inside or outside the house.

"What do you mean? What's going on?"

"Why, the preparations to move, of course," she said. She flourished a ring-laden hand in front of her face.

"So you're moving in with my father," said Patrick. It sounded stupidly obvious when he heard himself say it. He was relieved when Marie let it pass without comment.

She sat on one of the couches and gestured toward the other. Patrick took a seat and put his hands in his lap after trying a few self-conscious configurations of arm placement.

"So. What might I do for you, Patrick?" she asked, her smile an exact replica of her previous one, down to the angle at which she held her head.

If it was a defense, it was formidable. Patrick couldn't tell whether she was politely disinterested or intentionally inscrutable. Insignificant chatter had never come easily to him and, under these circumstances, it seemed impossible. He considered leaving, just standing up and walking out the door. Instead, he scrambled for a foothold.

"You and my father are pretty close," he managed. It was a bad start but he shrugged it off. "Does he seem different to you at all, lately?"

"In what way?" she asked.

Patrick could feel the beginnings of sweat form on his brow. "I don't know. We don't see each other that much, as you know," he said.

Her face neither confirmed nor denied any such knowledge.

"OK, well, do you remember the night at the Delacroix?"

"Are you referring to the night we got engaged?" she asked, the faintest hint of mirth playing at the corners of her mouth.

Patrick sighed. "Right. That does seem like something you'd remember," he said. He forced a laugh but any amusement Marie may have felt had already dried up and it seemed to Patrick as if her unflinching smile had begun to push outward from her, imposing its will on the room. He persevered nonetheless.

"He gave that speech and he talked about me and that—that just seemed strange for him," said Patrick.

"How so?"

"He doesn't usually talk about us in public."

Marie leaned in slightly but said nothing.

"Actually, he has never talked about us in public, not that I know of," said Patrick. He twisted one hand in the other and resolved to wait for Marie to speak no matter how uncomfortable the silence became.

She pushed him to the breaking point. The house stood still, not frozen but as if it she had muted it somehow, silenced all creaking floorboards and banished all ticking clocks, driven from the grounds any stray songbirds and even forbade the wind from rustling the trees. Long moments passed but Patrick held firm. Finally, she budged.

"You've spoken with your father about this matter, I presume?" she asked.

"Well, no," said Patrick.

"I see," she said. "I would certainly never presume to involve myself in the relationship between a father and a son. I'd suggest that you speak with him if you take issue with something he said."

"I wasn't clear," said Patrick. "It's not what he said that seems strange. Actually, that part sounded pretty familiar. It's that he said it in a speech to a roomful of people. I've never seen him do something like that."

"I see," said Marie. She leaned backwards until her back almost touched the couch cushion. "I'm afraid I've not seen your father give many speeches. I couldn't speak to whether or not his most recent one was unusual." The smile vanished. "But I wouldn't think you could, either. My understanding is that you haven't attended any of Henry's functions recently."

Patrick shifted in his seat.

"Not recently, no," he said. He opened his mouth to defend himself but was loathe to wade into his history with his father, particularly not with his father's new fiancée.

"Patrick, I believe you've come here to check up on me," said Marie.

He made a conscious effort not to allow his mouth to hang open. He knew he shouldn't be surprised; his efforts had been less than masterful. Yet he could not avoid the dawning suspicion that he had underestimated Marie.

"Oh, relax," said Marie. "You're not in trouble." She stood, patted Patrick's knee, and moved to the doorway, poked her head into the hallway and held up two fingers. She returned to the couch but stood behind it instead of sitting.

"I know my reputation," she said. "And you know that I've been married before. So ask your question."

Patrick smiled. Somewhere down the hallway, ice rattled into a glass.

"There doesn't seem to be much point to it now," he said.

"That's not a question," she said.

Patrick shrugged. He waved a hand toward the house at large. "It doesn't seem like you have much need for his money," he said.

The maid who'd greeted him at the door brought in two cocktail glasses on a tray. Marie took both and handed one to Patrick as the maid turned and left. The glass comforted him with its weight and its coldness, gave him something to hold, something to keep his hands occupied.

"That also is not a question," she said. "But you're correct. I do not have any need for his money."

Patrick took a sip, felt the comfortable bite warm his throat.

"You haven't been together very long," he said. "This seems a little fast, that's all."

"Patrick, neither your father nor I are young. We're obviously not planning to have children and money isn't a concern." She slid a pinkie out from under her glass and pointed it at Patrick. "Money isn't a concern for *either* of us, just to be clear. We care deeply for each other. We enjoy spending time together. There really isn't much more to consider than that. What would waiting longer do for either of us?"

She lifted her glass and drained it in a single, long sip.

"I see your point," said Patrick. "And you wouldn't tell me if you were only in it for the money, would you?"

She winked at him and smiled, a real smile that lifted her eyes and made her face move with a grace and ease that Patrick had never seen.

"Of course not," she said. "But ask me if I'd marry a poor man."

"Would you?"

"Oh, I think not. Who could afford the risk? I'm not saying that money isn't important. I'm saying that, while I'm not after your father's money, I know for certain that he is not after mine. We're a good match."

Softened a little by the whiskey and amused at how thoroughly he'd been bested, Patrick stood to leave.

"I won't take any more of your time," he said. He handed his glass to Marie.

"Before you go, I do have one question, if you'll indulge me," she said. "Do you know someone named Mary?"

"I don't think so," said Patrick.

"Your father has mentioned her a few times recently and I wondered if he was confusing me with someone else. Or if perhaps there was another woman."

Patrick smiled, but Marie was no longer smiling. He cleared his throat to change course. "Do you really think he'd talk to you about someone he was seeing on the side?"

"Oh, I'm kidding about it being another woman. I've heard him saying the name to himself a time or two, 'going to see Mary' or 'have to go see Mary.' When I ask him about it, he changes the subject."

"He talks to himself?" asked Patrick.

"I'm making this sound worse than it is," she said. "He doesn't mutter to himself like a crazy person. Just a word or two, now and then. Like people tend to do when they're by themselves."

"Wait, do you mean Mary as in his daughter Mary? Is that who he's talking about?"

"I wasn't aware that he had a daughter." For a fraction of a second, Patrick saw something in her eyes, a searching perhaps, or an unanswered question, a hint of a confession that she might not be as autonomous as she tried so hard to appear.

"He's never told you about her?" he asked. He tried to sound gentle.

"That would be something I'd remember, don't you think?" She drew herself to her full height and her face no longer held anything other than the mute, inexpressive smile she had worn when she entered the room.

"He had a daughter, years ago. Between me and Bryan."

"And where is this daughter now? Why haven't I met her?"

"She didn't make it. She died in the hospital, just a few hours after she was born." Patrick felt a momentary emptiness in his chest even though he had never met her.

Marie moved through the entryway, stood in the hall in a gestureless gesture toward the door. "I do thank you for stopping by. We'll have to do this again," she said, cordial once more though with a stiffness that he had not heard before. "As you can see, we're quite busy here."

Again, Patrick took note of the distinct absence of signs of life anywhere in the house. He moved past her toward the door. She followed, put a hand on the doorknob, but paused. Patrick waited, watched the unmoving hand, uncertain what to do.

"Tell me, are there any other O'Reilly children I don't know about?" she asked without looking at him.

"No," he said.

She opened the door.

"For what it's worth, I don't think he's ever really talked about her that much," he said, standing in sunlight and squinting into the doorway. "Mom talked about her sometimes and we said a prayer on her birthday, but that's it. I don't think he liked to talk about her. So maybe it's not strange that you didn't know about her."

"I thought he was mispronouncing my name," she said. "I just didn't know."

CHAPTER TWELVE

In the soft golden light of the late afternoon, the old man sat in the shade of the tree and watched the big man's arm swing over and over and each stroke of the hammer reverberated with a clap against the houses that lay on the other side of the creek. He swung with force and certainty but there was artistry in his motion, even if it was too violent and utilitarian to be graceful. The artistry was in the consistency, strength, and purposefulness with which the man plied his craft as his arm swung in the same violent, measured arc over and over again.

There was also skill. He was nailing boards to pilings planted in mud and, to do so, he had to balance himself atop the pilings or the boards he had already nailed and then, bending from the waist, maintain his precarious balance while swinging the hammer at a nail situated below his feet. It was an impressive display of power and agility, and it was clear that he had mastered his craft as he moved down the line working his way out over the water.

The old man did not know the names of the two smaller men. He could tell that they were Hispanic and that they worked well together, like a machine, precise and unrelenting. One of the two smaller men cut the boards in the yard and brought them out to be held in place and nailed in. In the deeper water, the other man stood in a johnboat to hold the boards.

They had a clever system and the old man wondered if it was their unique formula or if it was how everyone built docks. They started close to the yard, digging with shovels where it was above the waterline and using a high-pressure hose to blast into the underwater mud. Once they had a hole, they took a piling and rolled it out into the marsh or used a tether to drag it if it was too heavy. Then they used the crane to hoist it into the air.

It was the most dangerous part of the operation. Two of the men controlled the piling with ropes while it was lowered into the hole, but if the crane wasn't steady, the big piece of lumber swung like a pendulum, jerking the rope out of the men's hands or, if they were holding on too tight, dragging them across the mud. The crane was on a barge and thus bounced around if the wind gusted or the water grew choppy. Every once in a while, a boat traveling too fast in the waterway sent wake rolling into the creek that caused the barge to roll, the crane to sway, and the suspended piling to swing perilously. The crane, however, was operated with skill and patience and they avoided major accidents, at least during the couple of weeks he'd been watching.

The big guy, Patrick, always operated the crane. The old man liked Patrick. He was a broad-shouldered, soft-spoken kid whose youth still showed in his eyes despite the premature wrinkles in their corners. His crew was loyal to him; he could see it in how they responded when he spoke. Patrick reminded him of the men he had worked with years before, men who cared about the work more than they cared about talking about it. He missed the camaraderie and the purpose, the process of creating something with his hands, the sense of accomplishment at the end of the day. He had been a machinist in a factory that made metal parts for ships. In his teen years during World War II, when he was too young to enlist, he had worked on parts for submarines. Aside from putting his kids through school, his small part of the war effort was the thing about his work that had brought him the most pride.

He didn't really miss the work itself. Toward the end, his hands were worn out and his knuckles swollen with arthritis, and when it was time, he knew it was time and he walked away knowing he was lucky. His kids were happy and healthy, he and his wife had both managed to avoid the illnesses that had bogged down the lives of several of his friends, and he had the little house on the water with the big, wide tree out back. He didn't miss the work.

He had bought the house a few years after his youngest graduated from college, at a time when a working class man careful with his money could afford a cottage on the outskirts of what was then a gritty little fishing town. When it came time to retire, the choice was easy. They sold the house in Wilmington where they had lived for over thirty years and moved full-time into the little house on the water.

He was fortunate to have people his own age as neighbors, folks whose paths to the cottages were similar to his own. A few had been doctors and lawyers, but mostly they were like him, men who had worked with their hands and were caught by surprise when they had grown old. A couple of the houses were taken up by the trickle that would soon be a steady stream of successful younger people with young children who would buy up the houses at exorbitant prices when his own generation passed. These were not working class folks and their ideas of wealth and achievement differed from those of his generation. But the ones who had come already were nice enough and he didn't mind the younger set as much as some of his friends did. He hoped they wouldn't overdevelop the area as had been done in the beach front towns but, as far as he was concerned, no one had the right to tell anyone else where to live.

He wasn't exactly busy most of the time, but he had figured out how to keep boredom at bay without the structure of the workday. He played cards with his neighbors and fixed up the small things around the house that he could still handle. He and his wife went out to dinner once a week or sometimes had people over. He ran errands around town and spent as much time fishing as he could. New things, however, were rare, so when the men started working in the marsh behind his house, he was happy for the diversion.

In the early mornings, he sat on the deck. Later in the day, if it wasn't too hot, he pulled a chair under the big, wide tree and watched the men work, occasionally dozing off. He tried to stay out of their line of sight as much as possible; he didn't want them to think he was looking over their shoulder to be nosy or suspicious. But the men were out in the mud and busy with their work and they hardly seemed to notice him sitting there, peripherally sharing the satisfaction of their progress.

He knew the boy's father, or knew of him; they didn't exactly travel in the same circles. He respected Henry O'Reilly. He was good for the town.

The old man hadn't made the father-son connection at first. He had met Patrick through a referral from a neighbor who'd made no mention of who his father was. Nor had Patrick mentioned any connection to the most recognizable family in town. The old man had figured maybe he was a distant cousin, or perhaps the last name was a coincidence, but a friend told him the truth and it had surprised him. He wasn't sure why the son of such a man would choose this kind of work, but he admired that he did and wondered what the boy's father thought of his trade. He guessed that Henry O'Reilly was probably a little chafed that his son wasn't taking up the family business, but surely he had to be proud he had sought to make his own way, to leave his own mark on the world. If nothing else, Henry O'Reilly had raised a true and honest craftsman and they were rare as jewels. The old man knew that he'd have been proud of him if Patrick were his son.

His wife came out periodically to bring him something to drink or just to make sure he was still alive in that wooden deck chair that she kept telling him to leave on the deck but that he always dragged out under the tree anyway. She always offered the men something to drink as well, but they always politely declined. She knew her husband liked to watch them work; she knew he felt a connection with the big, sad-eyed young man.

She sensed her husband had lost something, that some sense of belonging and purpose had been left behind with "the fellas" when his career came to an end. It was something he was supposed to lose, something given up for something else the way one trades youth for children or independence for love. It was the natural order of things and her husband had borne it well and without regret, yet every now and then, even so many years later, she'd catch a faraway look in his eyes when he didn't think she was watching.

So she was happy when the men came to do the work and unwittingly gave her husband a chance to feel once more the energy of men working together and share, even if only by proxy, the fellowship of steady and hard-earned progress.

"Do you think they need a hand?" he had asked a couple of days ago, and she was careful not to smile. He caught himself and changed the subject.

She herself didn't pay much attention to the young men in the marsh. They seemed diligent and meticulous with their work, certainly, but it held no interest for her. It appeared mostly to be hot, difficult work in a filthy, unforgiving medium. But she appreciated what they did. It would be nice for her husband to be able to keep the boat so close to the house, and she cherished the prospect of their grandchildren playing on the dock, setting traps for crabs and trying to scoop minnows with a net.

The old man stirred at the touch of his wife's hand on his shoulder and she gave it a squeeze before moving back into the house. He did not know how long he had been asleep. The men were still working, but it must have been close to dinner time or his wife would not have woken him.

He stretched his legs and watched as Patrick, balancing atop a joist now far out over the water, swung downward in his practiced motion. The light was nearly lost. The day had come and gone, and a few of the sun's remaining rays silhouetted Patrick against the water and the marsh behind him.

An ease came over the old man, a warmth and calm that came sometimes when he thought about the end and what he would leave behind. There would be his family, of course, his children and grandchildren, and he took great comfort in knowing that he had given what he could for them. But there was something else, something he could not form into words or even a single coherent thought. It was something greater and more constant than lineage or family or anything that any one man might create. It was in the collective effort of all men and women, the massive, immeasurable sum of effort that had come together to build the world he knew. His world was built from brick and mortar, poured cement and welded metal and driven nails, knots that held cloth which conquered the seas and rivets that forged empires in the air.

Yet it was not the physical work alone, not something found in a turning wrench or spinning blade. For each ounce of sweat and pound of concrete poured into the earth, there were a thousand ideas. Ideas and improvements upon ideas and rebuilding after mistakes, and ideas to break the back of evil ideas, and despite all of the evil and the mistakes, they had built the country he loved. It was built by men and women; it was built by the old man and those he knew who had given their lives in war or in work to the cause and now, in his advancing age, he looked for it in the younger generations, looked for a man or woman who would pick up a hammer or a sword or a pen and stare hard-jawed and unflinching into the work of ages that built mankind and then put in his or her own day's work.

He looked out at Patrick.

The strong hands that held the hammer also held the world that he would leave behind, and he was comforted that the work still mattered and that men like Patrick came from men like him. There would always be work to be done, and he was pleased that there would always be those who would not shrink from that work. The old man looked out at the silhouetted young man and was grateful for his broad shoulders and the peace that came from the certainty that all that he would soon leave was in good hands.

CHAPTER THIRTEEN

"Did you ever think that perhaps it's not in your power to get me my job back?" Jack said as he handed Patrick a glass of sweet tea and took a seat next to him on the back deck of Jack's house.

Patrick shrugged.

"Patty, do you know why it's called 'Coastal Seafood' and not 'O'Reilly Seafood'?"

"It sounds less Irish. Although I'm not sure why that matters."

"There was a time, in this pernicious little corner of the world, when there were those who wouldn't do business with an Irish company. There was a lot of animosity about the Irish labor they'd brought in to build the bridge to the island. The Irish weren't Southern. Weren't white enough, according to a lot of folks, which never made any sense to me, but it's hard to rationalize bigotry. It's not as if Irish immigrants around here had it as bad as other people, but it was bad enough and it could have prevented your father's business from getting off the ground.

"This was well before I met your father. But, from everything I hear, he fought the idea of changing the name to something more bland, and fought it hard. Your grandfather was one of the immigrants who came here to work on that bridge. Your father must have felt like he'd be running away from his family if he changed the name. He was ready to say the hell with it and shove it in the face of anyone who disagreed with him. But you know who talked him into it?"

"Nope."

"Padraig O'Reilly. Your grandfather. He said it was just a name on a building. Said it was your dad's job to catch fish, not to make everyone less ignorant. Now, I don't know if there's a cause-and-effect relationship here or not, but Coastal Seafood is still here, and I'm guessing no one gives you much heat about your ancestry."

"So your point is that I should do my work and shut my mouth?" said Patrick.

"I have several points. First, before I was here, your father made sound decisions guided by the advice of someone other than me. Second, there's a chance that Sean can pull it together. Something might change. He might find his way to better advice. But my main point is this: There was a time when things were much more difficult for this company, when we were fighting for survival rather than just an increased market share. The company is stronger now. It will survive without me. So, in a long-winded way, yes, my point is that you should, as you put it, do your work and shut your mouth. Stay out of this mess. Stop trying to get my job back."

"Jack, it's not as if I quit my job and jumped in with both feet," said Patrick.

"You can't dabble in this sort of thing," said Jack. "And you sure as hell can't go rattling Bryan's cage like you did."

"More people need to rattle his cage, and they need to do it a lot harder than I did," said Patrick, miffed at the scolding. "And you're pretty damn protective of people who fired you."

"It's not them I'm worried about, Patty. It's you. You're the one who's going to get hurt. Sean and Bryan are what they are. You're the only one with something to lose."

"What could I possibly lose? They can't take anything from me."

"Oh yes they can," said Jack, "and you're fooling yourself if you think otherwise. Look, Patty, you're a very gifted carpenter. You *live* that job. You're good at something you love to do and you can make a living doing it. Do you know how rare that is?"

"Jack, I'm not quitting my job."

"Not the job itself, but the love of the job. That's what you could lose. That's what Sean can take from you. You wade in too deep and he'll suck the soul out of what you do every day."

"They'll ruin everything, Jack," said Patrick. "They'll chew on that company until there's nothing left and then they'll bankrupt this town. They'll ruin *everything*."

"If that's true, there's nothing you can do about it. There's no point in getting yourself dragged down with it."

"It wasn't long ago when you took me to a meeting because you felt I should be more involved. What happened to that idea?"

"As a member of the family, you deserved to be informed. Your level of involvement was your choice. But things have changed. I'm not there anymore. For that matter, neither is your father. Say what you will about him, he was never threatened by you. I'm not sure that's true of your brothers. Particularly after you talked to Bryan like that."

"Oh, what's Bryan going to do?"

"Nothing, I'm sure. His wife, however, is the most dangerous person involved. She has way too much at stake and way too little of herself at risk."

"See, Jack, that's exactly why you need to be involved. You could do something about her."

"I really can't, Patty. My job is to assist your father, regardless of what form that takes."

"You're sure as hell not assisting him now, are you?"

"I check in on your father every day. How often do you get over to his house?" Jack said, his tone even, direct.

"I didn't mean to imply anything," said Patrick. "Do you really visit him every day?"

Jack nodded. He walked to the rail and looked out at the water. Jack's house was larger and his lawn wider than Patrick's, but the backdrop was the same. They lived within a couple miles of each other, both on the same side of the waterway.

"Are you really this comfortable with being fired?" asked Patrick.

"Do you know how many people I've had to fire during my career? It's not as if I didn't realize that the blade could swing back at me. It'd be a bit unfair to wring my hands now and cry foul."

"But you were fired unfairly and for a stupid reason," said Patrick. "The people you fired were fired for cause, right?"

"Oh, most of them. But there were some that had to be moved for financial reasons. Some were personality conflicts. Some got fired just because your father didn't trust them. I didn't get to decide whether it was right or wrong. It's the ability to pull the trigger that counted, not how I felt afterwards."

"Do you ever regret it? All those people you put out of work?"

"No. Someone had to do it. I didn't like doing it, which is why I was good at it. Better coming from me than someone who might have enjoyed it. If nothing else, I treated people with respect."

"So, you do resent what happened."

"I do not feel that my work was concluded satisfactorily. I was not able to leave in a manner I would have chosen. And I do not feel that my dismissal was a sound decision for the company. But we live in a town where a lot of working careers end in seaside memorials. You make the best of what you get and count yourself lucky if you walk away in one piece."

Patrick looked skeptically at Jack, who smiled and continued.

"In terms of finances, I haven't needed to work for quite a while, if that's what you're worried about. Your father has never been reluctant about rewarding his employees for their loyalty and service. And as I said, I knew my dismissal was a possibility. I planned accordingly."

"No, it's not that. I'm not talking about money," said Patrick. "But I do have a hard time believing you're so comfortable with how little your life's work is being rewarded."

"I don't feel like my work is over yet."

"You're saying you'd go back? Are you going to try to get back in?"

"Patty, I need you to listen to me very carefully. I consider it my task to advise and assist Henry O'Reilly in whatever way I can. I believe that he is responsible for the well-being of this town and I know for a fact that he's responsible for my success. My service to your father, however, need not be in a formal context, under the employ of Coastal Seafood or otherwise. So I do not need you to make any further efforts to get me hired back at a company where Henry O'Reilly is no longer working. Is that clear? Can I trust you to respect my wishes in this matter?"

Patrick held his hands up in concession.

"Fine," he said. "I'm certainly not going to do anything you don't want me to. I just don't understand what I'm supposed to do now."

"You go back to work, Patty. That's what you do."

"At least I know what the hell I'm doing out there," he said, jerking his head toward the water beyond the lawn. They sat in silence and watched the marsh birds dart across the mud flats left exposed by the retreating tide.

"So, how is he?" asked Patrick.

"He's okay," said Jack. "He's a little . . . perturbed with how things have gone since he left."

"What do you mean, 'he left'? Where's he gone?"

"You haven't heard?"

"Nobody tells me anything."

"Your father doesn't spend much time at the office anymore. He mostly stays home."

"Why?"

Jack looked sharply at Patrick.

"I wouldn't wade too deep into this," said Jack. "It's the natural order of things after a power shift. With Sean running things, your father doesn't feel the need to be there as much."

"Doesn't feel the need to be there or isn't allowed in the building?" asked Patrick.

"No, nothing like that. It's not as if Sean can ban him from the premises. But a few overturned decisions, a few embarrassing displays of power by Sean, and the point was well made. He doesn't go there much anymore."

"You mean without you there, no one will support him. Everyone's afraid of Sean."

"Again, Patty, it's the natural order of things. Deposed kings don't sit next to the new king."

"Jesus, that happened fast," said Patrick.

"It's the way of the world, son," said Jack. "Just the way it is."

"Why are you trying to calm me down?" asked Patrick, triggered by a softness around the edges of Jack's words.

"I'm concerned that this news is going to cause you to pursue the matter further—that you're going to show up at Sean's door like you did at Bryan's."

"I'm not mad. It's not like I'm thrilled at the way things have gone. I'm surprised, but I guess this was inevitable. I just never thought I'd see the day when the old man wasn't at the helm. I mean, if ever anyone was the job he worked, it was my father."

"I can understand your surprise," said Jack, his voice flat, almost detached. He was staring straight ahead at a spot somewhere out over the water, and Patrick saw a muscle in his jaw twinge. When Jack saw him watching, his face relaxed and he stood abruptly.

"Well, Patty, thank you for stopping by. Please remember what I've asked of you. Please do not pursue this matter."

On the road back to his house, Patrick tried to unravel the conversation from the beginning to pinpoint the change in Jack's demeanor. He wished he were more perceptive. He had spent much of his life conscientiously avoiding close interaction with people and the concrete downside of that was making itself known. He suspected, however, that even if he had acquired the ability to analyze people and draw usable conclusions from them, Jack had honed the art of intentional inscrutability over a large number of years.

Loose ends and fragments of conversation flickered in his mind as he drove. In the hope that an answer might occur to him if he kept driving, he opted not to go home. Instead, he continued along the main road that led out of town. Not far beyond the turnoff to his house, the road veered inland as it headed north and widened at the outskirts of town.

As he drove, a creeping sadness gradually displaced his ruminations. He felt as if an era had passed and no one had taken any note of its passing. Coastal Seafood had been a constant in his life and his father had been such an integral part of that constant that no matter the inevitability of the change, the magnitude of the shift was such that its tremors shook Patrick despite his distance from the epicenter.

Almost as astounding as the tidal shift in management of the company that permeated all of Spring Tide was the nonchalance of those closest to it. He understood Sean; Sean operated under a massive sense of entitlement and there was little else needed to understand him. Bryan, gutless and handcuffed though he was, still had to be capable of at least registering surprise or sentimental reflection, yet he had shown neither. Jack, who had perhaps lost the most, seemed downright philosophical about the whole affair. Even the town itself had scarcely reacted. There was no buzz, no sound from the periphery of the town, no whispers from barstools or inside corner stores. It was as if the town refused to believe anything other than that the man's being alive was all that mattered. Patrick felt as if he was writing an epitaph for his father's working career that no one was interested in reading, and an abiding loneliness accompanied the thought.

Preoccupied, he drove far beyond the edge of town, past a barren stretch of pine trees that was home only to the road, an occasional gas station, and a small handful of forlorn single-story motels. He turned into the parking lot of one of the motels to turn around. As he looped through, he saw only a few cars, most of which were suitably shabby to match the general appearance of the motel. Two cars, however, were conspicuously shiny and clean. The cars—a sleek black sedan and a convertible coupe—were parked next to each other, and Patrick figured it was a little obvious what the owners of the cars were doing in such a place at such an hour.

As he turned onto the road, movement in the corner of his eye caught his attention and he looked back. The door in front of the cars opened and Sean emerged from a darkened room and strode briskly toward the black sedan.

CHAPTER FOURTEEN

It's none of my business.

I have to know.

A decision was made with a jerk of the wheel and a screech of the tires.

He stood on the blacktop of the parking lot and let the early summer heat bear down upon him. Sweat beaded on his forehead and ran down his neck. His lips curled. An image of Suzanne refused to leave his mind. He forced himself not to think of the children.

The brazenness was irritating to him, the arrogance of not even bothering to hide, their cars left right out in front where they could be seen from the road. The cliché also irritated him, the afternoon encounter at the seedy motel and the lack of creativity of it all. What he felt most sharply, however, was an enormous, untamed fury at being witness to the event, at being in the position of having to decide what to do with what he had seen.

Eventually, he looked down and saw a small puddle on either side of him from the sweat sliding down his arms and dripping off the knuckles of his clenched fists. With nowhere to direct his hands and no reason to punish himself in the abandoned parking lot, he climbed into the Jeep and drove home.

The drive to the motel became Patrick's ritual, his obsession. He made the drive every day at the same hour of the afternoon. He had no plan for when he caught Sean. He knew of no real action he could take against him, aside from telling his wife, but Patrick was pretty sure that would punish Suzanne far more than it would Sean. He felt caged by his awareness, and until he could confront the author of his torment, he could do nothing but stalk the dingy motel by the side of the road.

The daily trip became the focus of his life, the center of his day, so much so that he began leaving work early to perform the ritual and, daily, left José and Javier bewildered by his strange behavior.

Then he caught him.

The same two cars, parked in the same place in front of the same room. He stopped behind Sean's car and considered his options. His initial instinct was to drive his Jeep into the back of Sean's car, force it through the curtained front window of the motel room, and catch the two in the act in spectacular fashion. Or he could hide and observe the two of them as they left, an approach that might be best in case of the unlikely event that there was a reasonable explanation for Sean's presence at the motel.

Ultimately, the dry, hard lump in his throat demanded a more direct approach. He backed the car away and parked outside the line of sight of the room's window. He waited.

After an hour, Sean emerged. Patrick approached him from behind. As Sean opened the door of his car, Patrick kicked it shut and the handle snapped out of Sean's hands.

Sean looked up wild-eyed, his hand still outstretched. He didn't seem to register who he was looking at.

"I will give you one chance," said Patrick, holding up a quivering finger, "to tell me who is in that room right now."

Sean showed no signs of having heard him. He stared open-mouthed at Patrick, cemented to the ground like frightened prey whose only chance for survival was to remain motionless.

Patrick slammed his fist down on the hood of Sean's car as hard as he could. It made a sound like a shot. Sean blinked several times in rapid succession.

"Answer me, Sean."

"Whoa, Patty, take it easy. You dented it."

"Answer me. Who is in that room?"

"That's not really your business," said Sean, without conviction. Then he shook his head as if trying to wake himself and spoke louder, facing the door from which he had emerged: "It's not your business who is in that room."

"Come on, Sean. I'm getting in there whether you warn whoever it is or not."

"She'll never open the door for you," said Sean.

"You're caught. You need to tell me who's in there," said Patrick. He could feel the heat rise in his chest and his periphery narrowed around Sean's face.

"Forget it, Patty. It's none of your damn business and she's not opening that door."

"Fine. Go to hell," said Patrick. He stepped up to the door, gave it one hard kick and the door flew open. Wood splintered out from the jamb. He saw her, more shape than person as his eyes adjusted to the darkness. She was frozen, half-cowering against the back wall with her shirt barely around her shoulders. It took a moment for her features to become clear.

Helen recognized him before he recognized her. The abject terror from the door frame shattering was already draining from her, but her face still registered a substantial amount of shock, along with a much different kind of fear from a moment before.

"Wait," said Patrick, holding his hand up, his palm facing Helen although she was making no effort to move. "Wait. Just wait."

Sean came up behind him and Patrick held his other hand up. He was standing between the two. Neither Helen nor Sean spoke, but neither moved either, as if Patrick held them motionless with an overwhelming, unseen force directed from his palms.

"What is this?" asked Patrick finally. "I don't understand."

Sean looked around Patrick at Helen. She shrugged at him and finished buttoning her shirt. She had managed to pull on her skirt. Her feet were bare. She made a passing effort at smoothing her hair, then crossed her arms across her chest and thrust out her chin.

"What don't you understand, Patrick?" she asked. "What part are you having trouble with?"

"No, no, no," said Patrick. "This can't be."

"All right," said Sean, "Let's all just settle down."

"What have you done, Sean?" asked Patrick.

"Take it easy, Patty," said Sean. "Let me try to explain."

Patrick gesticulated wildly around the room.

"Look where we are! What's to explain?"

"You're right. But you have to understand that there are other people involved here, even if they don't know about this. I need you to be careful," said Sean.

"What the hell are you talking about, Sean? There's nobody else involved. There's nobody else in the world right now. There's only you two assholes cheating on your spouses with each other in this shitty motel room."

"You know," said Helen to Sean, "there's a good chance no one will believe him. We could discredit him. Think what his reputation is right now."

"You shut your mouth," said Patrick, wheeling on Helen and pointing a finger at her face. "Whatever the hell you're talking about, you shut your mouth."

"You can't talk to her like that, Patrick," said Sean.

Patrick gripped Sean by the shoulders and shoved him into the wall with such force that it shook behind him.

"If you get to fuck my brother's wife, I get to say whatever the hell

I please," said Patrick.

"Let's just take it easy," said Sean, his back still against the wall, his eyes wide but his voice calm. "I know what this looks like, but just hear me out. There are important ramifications for all of us."

"You have a *wife*, Sean. You have kids. You both have kids. You . . ." His voice trailed off as the import of what he had just said struck him. He sagged onto the bed behind him and rubbed the back of his neck.

"My God," said Patrick. "What about the kids? They'll never get over this. What's going to happen with the kids?"

"Nothing is going to happen with the kids," said Sean as he pulled himself erect and straightened his clothes. "Because we're not going to tell anyone about this."

"You're out of your mind."

"What good would it do, Patty? Do you think Bryan wants to know? Do you think he wants to be put in the middle of this situation? And how about Suzanne? Do you think her life will be better or worse if you tell her? And you said it yourself. The kids wouldn't get over this."

"It's not my fault you did this, Sean. You should have thought about all of that before you started banging this whore," said Patrick, jerking his thumb over his shoulder toward Helen.

"Excuse me?" said Helen.

"Where are we right now?" asked Patrick, spreading his arms outward. "Where are we, Helen? What are we doing here, huh?"

Helen started to speak, thought better of it, and looked away.

"You know, Patty, she's not wrong," said Sean. "We could probably deny this. We could make it seem like you're making it all up. But I'd rather it not come to that. I'd rather not have to dirty your name in this town. You have to understand something. What you've got here is a little bit of leverage. The question is, what are you going to do with it?"

"You can't be serious."

"Of course I am. If you can look beyond the emotion of the moment, you'll see that this is just a negotiation. That's all it is. I, for example, don't want this . . . episode, shall we say, discussed outside of this room. I also don't want to have to destroy my brother's reputation. What do you want?"

"I want you to give the company back to Dad and I want Helen to kill herself," said Patrick.

"Be serious."

"I've never been more serious."

"Come on, Patty. What do you want? You want back in, maybe? You want the slice of the pie you lost when Dad started handing out shares?"

"Sean, what are you doing?" asked Helen.

"I'm just trying to find out what Patrick here is interested in. Come on, Patty. What's your price?"

"I don't have a price."

"If that's true, you're the only one. Come on. What's it going to take? Personally, I thought you were just as deserving as Bryan. What's he really bringing to the table?"

"I don't think you should be offering such things to him," said Helen.

"You want it all for yourself, right, Helen?" asked Sean with a condescending grin. "Name your price, Patrick. Come on."

Patrick thought of Jack, of the job he had lost, and he couldn't help seeing the opportunity dangled before him. He remembered what Jack had told him, but Jack could not have predicted such a circumstance. Considering Sean's offer, however, made Patrick feel nothing but doubt and a vague nausea.

"I don't want anything from either of you," said Patrick.

"You don't want anything. So you'd tell Bryan about this? You'd ruin his life out of spite? You'd destroy your niece and nephews' lives just to feel superior? Just to stick it to your big brother?"

"You're a son of a bitch. It's not my fault you did this," said Patrick, keeping his face wooden so as not to reveal the sinking ache he felt for the children, for Suzanne, and even for Bryan.

"I'll give you something else to think about," said Sean, as if the entire discussion was nothing more than a hypothetical. "This kind of scandal would rock this town. It'd be bad for business. Our employees are already on edge with Dad stepping down. This sort of thing could cause a panic."

"So I should forget what I've seen for the town's sake?"

"I think it might be a good idea for you to think of somebody other than yourself."

"Tell me this, Sean. What could possibly give you the right to tell me what's best for this town? Or for anybody?"

"As usual, I don't think you're looking at the big picture," he said. "There's risk for you, too. If you leak this and Bryan gets off his dead ass long enough to file for divorce, chances are good that Helen winds up with half his share. Which means that she and I would, between the two of us, have a majority. Is that what you want?"

"Sean! Why are you telling him that?" demanded Helen.

"Hey, he wants a seat at the big boy table. I'm just shooting straight with him."

"It's equally true of you, you know," said Helen. "If your wife divorces you, she'd wind up with half of your share."

"My wife isn't going to leave me," said Sean. "Besides, I've got a pre-nup. Do you have a pre-nup, Helen?"

Color rose in Helen's cheeks. Her lips pressed tightly together. But Sean continued.

"Tell you what, Patty. You agree not to tell anyone about this, and I'll see to it that you get half of Bryan's share. How'd that be?"

"You son of a bitch!" shrieked Helen. "That's not yours to give away! What belongs to Bryan belongs to *me*."

Patrick shook his head and blinked as if to wake himself.

"Enough!" he thundered and the force of his voice made Sean and Helen recoil. Both looked at Patrick as if he had just materialized in the room.

"Is this really all you care about?" asked Patrick. "Is there nothing else in this world for either of you but money and damage control and shares of a company that neither of you deserve? Don't you care at all about your family? Christ, Sean, this is your brother's *wife*. What the hell's the matter with you? Do either of you have any sense of morality? Honor? Pride, for God's sake?"

Helen showed neither guilt nor remorse. She seemed, if anything, irritated by the interruption. Sean looked at Patrick as if his entire outburst had been spoken in a foreign language.

"So where does this leave us?" Sean asked.

Patrick, agape, stared at him.

"You're the worst person I know," said Patrick quietly. "That's where this leaves us."

He brushed past Sean and walked out. Behind him, Sean stuck his head around the door.

"Does this mean you're going to tell—"

"I don't know, goddammit!" shouted Patrick. "But I'm not making any deals."

He strode past the telltale cars, stopped, turned around, and kicked the driver's side mirror of Sean's car. It flew off and rattled across the pavement. Patrick looked at Sean, challenging him. Sean shook his head but said nothing, so Patrick turned and left.

As he drove home, the full weight of what had happened settled in and his stomach churned. He pulled the car over, fell onto his hands and knees, and vomited. He wiped his mouth with the back of his hand and sat up, oblivious to the curious faces in the windows of the passing cars.

A profound sense of loss overwhelmed him, a strange mix of uncertainty, desperation, and futility. Regardless of the low opinion he had always held of Sean, Patrick had assumed, or at least hoped, that there was something of substance beneath it all. But in a dingy motel by the side of the road, he had found that it had all been a lie he told himself. The driving force behind Sean's aggressive and often ill-advised tactics was simple, pedestrian lust. Or lust coupled with greed, or with extravagant laziness, or any of the other empty things that were the hallmarks of soft hands holding unearned wealth.

The undeniable conclusion was that he had one brother lost in his own apathy and another awash in his own corporeal satisfaction. The company was supposed to be theirs. But there was no one at the helm.

Eventually, he pulled himself off the ground and climbed behind the wheel. He drove home because he had nowhere else to go. He had run out of people to talk to and wouldn't have known what to say even if he hadn't.

Although it made his chest hurt and his hands shake, he conceded that he had lost. His brother had called his bluff, without even being aware that he was doing so, by underscoring a fact that was the same before Patrick had entered the room as it was after: Patrick was a decent person and Sean was not. He would not be able to bring himself to tell Bryan or Suzanne what he had seen. He knew that Sean had sought to negotiate so that he could tether Patrick to the thing he had done, could make him an accessory, because, in Sean's mind, both parties being dirty was as good as both being clean. By the same logic, he knew that Sean wouldn't understand that his youngest brother wasn't a threat to him, that Patrick could not bring himself to hurt innocents but Sean could, and that disparity kept Sean's secret safe.

CHAPTER FIFTEEN

A knock on the door compelled Patrick to get up. It was nearly ten in the morning and, though he had been awake for hours, he had not yet made it out of bed. The knocking irritated him, but he was grateful to have something external on which to focus. He rose, pulled on some pants, and answered the door, where he found Javier and José smiling nervously at him.

"You are sick?" asked Javier.

"What?"

"You are sick? If you are sick, we go home and come back mañana. But you didn't show up and we worried," said Javier.

"Oh. Shit. Sorry," said Patrick. "Not sick. Sleeping." He placed his cheek on the back of his hand. "Sleeping."

Javier's brow creased. He said something to José in Spanish, then said in English, "We worried. We showed up at job this morning and no boss. José says trabajamos, but I say no, we'll come find the boss first." He looked at José again, then added, "We worried. Both of us worried."

"Sorry, guys. I was just . . . never mind. Something came up and I was up late. We'll go right now. Trabajamos ahora. Okay?"

"Okay," said José. "You are okay? Not sick?"

"No. Not sick. I'm fine. Let me get dressed and we'll go."

Javier nodded and translated to José. José asked him something and Javier said something back and nodded in a reassuring manner as he spoke.

He was happy to be at work once he got into the rhythm of the day. The job was physics and chemistry and geometry. The rest of the world was a gray void in which nothing was certain or constant. He felt betrayed in a sense, that he had braced against the indecipherable fickleness and disloyalty of people and been let down by them despite his caution.

The only conclusion he had drawn that morning had been the hastily assembled and impractical working theory that neither bad things nor bad people were to be found within his house, so he would just stay there. In retrospect, however, he was glad that José and Javier had come for him.

They worked long and well and, when their shadows stretched far along the joists of the dock, they stopped for the day. The men gave him a ride home.

He was still standing at his front door after they left when a car parked on the street a couple houses away started up and pulled into the driveway.

Patrick did not recognize the car and couldn't see who was driving. He wasn't sure whether he should go inside or wait for the interloper to approach him. He was relieved, if baffled, when the car door opened and Doug Castin stepped out.

Doug was of average height but lean and slightly stooped at the shoulder, so he seemed smaller than he was. He moved in a jangly, loose-limbed manner, as if his appendages had been attached haphazardly and in great haste. He approached the steps without offering the faintest acknowledgment, and Patrick wasn't sure that Doug had seen him at all, even when he came to a stop at the bottom step.

"Good evening, Mr. O'Reilly. My name is Doug Castin. Perhaps you remember me," said Doug in an unpunctuated, arrhythmic manner that sounded as if he were reading something uninteresting out loud.

"Call me Patrick, Dougie. Doug. Of course I remember you. We've known each other for the better part of a decade."

"I wasn't sure you would because we haven't spoken in several years and we were never friends," he said with neither malice nor resentment.

"To be fair, I don't have a lot of friends," said Patrick. "And you're quite a bit younger than I am. But you've been working for my father since you were a kid mowing his lawn, so I remember you, even if we're not friends."

Doug looked up at Patrick out of dark, deep-set, heavily-browed eyes. Patrick was surprised by the intensity of the gaze given that the rest of him seemed rather slumped.

"Your father has been very good to me," Doug said.

"Sure. I'm sure he has been," said Patrick.

Doug nodded. Patrick nodded back. He looked expectantly at Doug. Doug looked back at him.

"So, Doug," Patrick said, long after awkwardness had set in, "what can I do for you?"

"Are you prepared for the coming storm?" asked Doug.

"Say that again?"

"Are you prepared for the coming storm?"

Patrick looked at Doug. There were no context clues in either speech or mannerism.

"What storm is that, Doug?"

"There's a tropical storm nearing the Caribbean. It's predicted to come up the coast."

"I hadn't heard. But it's awfully early in the season for anything major. I'm sure we'll be fine. Is that why you came here? To warn me about a storm a thousand miles away?"

"No, sir. I simply noticed that you didn't seem to be preparing."

"Well, this is about as prepared as I get. The houses on the island take the brunt of the storms, and if any windows get blown out, I'm pretty confident I can replace them. I don't mean to be rude, but what are you doing here, aside from weather warnings?"

"Aren't you going to invite me in?"

"Sure, I guess. You bet. Come on in," said Patrick, pushing open the door behind him.

"I'm sorry to be so insistent," said Doug once the door was closed. "It's not wise that I be seen here."

Patrick looked critically at the unusual young man who stood before him. He tried not to appear amused, but he could not imagine any reason why anyone might care where Doug was seen.

"Are you in some kind of trouble?" asked Patrick.

"Certainly not physical danger, I assume," said Doug. "But there would be great displeasure at the office if I were seen here."

"Won't they recognize your car out front?"

"I don't imagine anyone knows what kind of car I drive," he responded, "but I borrowed a friend's car just to be safe."

"It's a small town, Doug. People probably know your social security number and pants size."

"A valid point. I'll be brief then," said Doug. "It's Alzheimer's disease."

"What is?" Patrick asked, but he knew. His chest thumped hollow and the hair on the back of his neck stood up.

"Wait," said Patrick. "Just wait."

Doug took a small step back, clasped his hands behind his back, and did as he was asked. A full minute passed.

"How do you know? How long have you known? *Why* do you know, Doug?" asked Patrick.

"Those are fair questions," said Doug, "First, I'd like to apologize for being the one to break the news to you. I know we don't know each other very well, Mr. O'Reilly."

"Doug, for the love of God, call me Patrick. You've just told me how my father is going to die. I think we should be on a first-name basis."

"Certainly, sir. As you wish."

"How long have you known?"

"The diagnosis was made a little more than six months ago."

"And it's definitely Alzheimer's? It's not something else? It's not, I don't know—"

"It's Alzheimer's disease. A specialist in Durham confirmed it."

Jessica. Jennifer.

Unbidden, the idea took shape, expanded, eclipsed any doubt. He bent at the waist and put his hands on his knees, stared at the floor. The idea had taken something more than his breath, but he knew he wouldn't be able to get whatever it was back so he kept his hands on his knees and tried to catch his breath because that, at least, was something he could do.

"Who knows about this?" asked Patrick, once he had regained the strength to stand upright again.

"Only myself, Mr. Kent, and the doctors. And your father, of course. And now you."

"Sean and Bryan?"

"No. Mr. Kent did not think that would be wise."

"Marie?"

"We can assume that your father told her. Mr. Kent is certain we can count on her discretion. She'd have nothing to gain by sharing the information."

"No offense, Doug, but why do *you* know?"

"I am senior assistant to your brother Sean." Patrick squinted at Doug. Doug looked back at him.

"But you said Sean doesn't know. Might be time to explain yourself, Doug," said Patrick, "before I throw you out of this house."

"Of course. I should have explained myself more thoroughly at the outset. Previously, I was assistant to your father and worked directly under Mr. Kent. Upon Mr. Kent's dismissal, I wanted to leave as a show of solidarity. Mr. Kent, however, saw value in me staying on. Your brother evidently did not perceive me as a threat and kept me on as his chief assistant."

"So you are to Sean what Jack was to my father?"

"In title, yes. But I'm afraid that neither Sean nor I are adequate substitutes for our predecessors."

"And you relay information to Jack without Sean knowing?"

"I do."

"That seem like the right thing to do?"

"It does. My allegiances are to your father and to Mr. Kent, in that order. I've made my decision and chosen my side. I stand by my decision."

Patrick eyed Doug. He was certain he had underestimated the odd young man who stood in his kitchen. He noticed that, despite his frail and oddly-assembled build, Doug did not stand like a man who lacked confidence. There was no bravado in his stance, but neither was there fear or hesitation.

"Well, it's no wonder you're worried about people seeing you here then," said Patrick.

"Indeed, sir. But they'd be watching you, not me."

"Yeah, right. I doubt anyone's interested in what I'm doing."

"Your brother hired a private investigator to do just that," said Doug.

"Get the hell out of here."

"I sat in on the meeting."

"But why?" asked Patrick. "He's my brother, for Christ's sake."

"He's looking for an angle. Anything he can use. You're an unknown. He doesn't know anything about you and that scares him. Nothing makes a paranoid person more nervous than the unknown."

Patrick rubbed his furrowed brow and looked down at the floor. He was angry, certainly, but he was surprised to find that stronger than anger was a pervasive sadness, a sense of isolation and distance and detachment that made him pull his arms tightly around himself.

"How long's this been going on?" he asked.

"Ever since you went to Bryan's house."

Patrick nodded. In a very short span of time, he had found that his father was losing his mind and that Sean was having him investigated. He struggled to reconcile himself with the two cumbersome loads.

"Sir, if I may?"

Patrick looked up. "Right, sure," he said. "Go ahead."

"I came here to give you this." He handed Patrick a business card.

"Who is this?"

"It's the doctor in Durham, the specialist. He'll return your calls."

"Why would I call him? You don't think I believe you?"

Doug shifted his weight from one foot to the other. It was the first uncomfortable movement he had made.

"We believe that when your father signed the contract that endowed your brothers with ownership of the company, he was not of sound mind."

"Who's 'we'?"

"Mr. Kent and I," said Doug. "We disagree, however, on what to do about it. He wanted you left out of this altogether. I thought that you should have all the available information. I came here against his wishes. But I didn't lie to him. He knows I'm here."

"What would you have me do with this information?"

"That, Mr. O'Reilly, is entirely up to you."

"Oh, come on, Doug. Surely you have something in mind. I doubt you risked life and limb or whatever else just to come here and give me a piece of paper with a guy's name on it."

"I've presented you with all the information I have. I felt that was my duty, and I've fulfilled it."

"So you have no opinion on what I should do?"

"None that I wish to share," said Doug.

"I assume you're talking about some sort of legal action, but you need to know that I'm not good with that sort of thing. I wouldn't know where to start. I wouldn't even know what I'd be asking a lawyer to do."

Doug shrugged but said nothing.

"If you want me to use this as leverage against Sean, you're out of your mind. I don't trust him to hold up his end of any deal we'd make."

Still Doug said nothing.

"Well, if you won't tell me what you think I should do, will you at least tell me why you won't?"

"It's not my place. It's a difficult decision, and it's yours to make. You're his son."

"Look, if you're thinking I might make some move to replace Sean, you may as well forget it. It's not happening. Jack should have told you that."

"He has told me precisely that," said Doug.

"Well, good," said Patrick, more fiercely than he intended, but Doug's countenance did not register any change. "So thanks, Doug, for telling me all this. I appreciate your candor."

"No thanks necessary," said Doug flatly, turning to leave. "It was the right thing to do."

Somewhere off in the same dark night, in the general direction Patrick faced as he watched Doug's retreating taillights, a massive jagged cloud spun like a saw-blade, gathering itself around its center as it inched closer to a distant Caribbean shore where people Patrick would never meet braced against the longest of nights.

CHAPTER SIXTEEN

The storm and Patrick waited. Anthony came ashore on the Windward Islands but bounced back into the Atlantic, where it inexplicably stood offshore, hovering somewhere between a tropical storm and a hurricane and showing no indication of moving on. The storm had been predicted to follow the coast from the ocean side of Florida and work its way north; failing that, it would drift into the ocean, lose momentum, and fall apart. It did neither. Instead, it spun around itself indecisively for days and sent paroxysms of rain and wind across the islands of the Caribbean.

Patrick, too far north to yet feel any of its effects, knew the damage the storm could do and resolutely set his crew to burying hurricane anchors on the Macready dock. The anchors were long, sturdy screws that bored deep into the mud, the eye threaded with heavy-gauge wire which was then wrapped around the joists in the hopes that a storm surge would flood the dock but not be able to lift it free and destroy it. Although far from perfect, the screws offered the best chance for a dock's survival against a hurricane.

His life was spent both protecting against and profiting from the hurricanes that tormented the East Coast—an irony that did not escape him. The big ones, the storms of legends and nightmares, fracture islands, vaporize beaches, and drown entire cities. No formula of wood and nails can fend off a direct hit. So he built his docks strong and set them hard into the earth, and when the winds died and the damage was tallied, Patrick was among those called to put the pieces back together. His goal, his perverse unreachable goal, was to put himself out of business.

For the most part, his work remained intact. A direct hit was rare. Every ten years or so, a hurricane might come ashore near Spring Tide, and usually once it did, it had strayed so far from the nurturing warm waters of the Caribbean that it had lost much of its energy. The Outer Banks to the north were more frequent targets due to the angle at which they protruded into the storms' paths, but life-altering storms were not common here. Most of Patrick's work involved replacing poorly constructed or aging and rotted docks that came apart during more routine storms.

Setting the hurricane anchors was the next step anyway, and with a storm of unknown force looming, Patrick poured himself into his work with a nearly unsustainable intensity. He still did not think Anthony would amount to much in his part of the world, but he respected the storms too much to assume anything. So while Anthony bided its time, Patrick worked.

During the work, however, he was waiting. Every morning, he walked past the doctor's business card that sat in the same spot on the kitchen counter where Patrick had put it after Doug left. Every evening, well past nightfall, Patrick walked past the card again. In the time between, he considered what to do about it. And he waited, waited to decide, waited until the next morning, waited to see what might happen. He was not sure if his work kept him from pursuing the matter or if he was using the work to distract him from it. He did know, however, that his work was the priority, the variable that could be controlled, affected, and brought to a successful conclusion.

On the fourth day, word came that the storm had broken free from its stalemate with the Gulf Stream and was headed north. It was unclear whether it would follow the coast northward or enter the Gulf of Mexico; the forecasters were unable to come up with a definitive prediction.

They did, however, officially upgrade the storm to a hurricane. It was somehow gaining strength despite having languished for days in the tropics.

When Patrick heard the news of the storm's movement, he was waist-deep in mud and he looked instinctively at the sky. The sky did not tip its hand. It was blue and nearly cloudless and the only giveaway was the slight coolness in the air, due perhaps to the low-pressure system that might lure the storm closer. He stopped for a moment and looked back toward land. A light breeze teased at the treetops beyond the houses. Otherwise, all was calm. He could understand how, in the days before modern forecasting technology, entire villages, even cities, were caught unaware by the lurking giants and then laid unceremoniously to waste.

He considered what he knew, what he had seen of the storms and the water over the course of his life. It was early in the season. Too early, perhaps, for Anthony to survive for long if it went north. If the storm chose a path toward Spring Tide, it would probably be fairly toothless by the time it came ashore. Regardless, he would prepare. He would drive the anchors, he would tie the lines.

As Patrick slept that night, the storm, gathered in a tight fist, edged out into the Atlantic just far enough to get pushed east of the Florida Keys. By morning, it was off the coast of Miami and headed north. With every mile it travelled, its chances of passing Spring Tide by diminished. Unless it veered inland uncharacteristically early, it would follow the coast north until it came ashore or dissolved.

Patrick heard the forecast on his way to work the next morning, but he could feel it in the town. People were gathered in small groups engaged in intense discussion. More than a few cars passed Patrick on their way out of town with kids strapped in seats and luggage stacked high in the back. Fishermen scurried around docked boats along the wharf, retying lines and double-checking backup bilge systems. An unusually large number of people were on the town docks, staring out at the water. Everybody seemed to have one eye on the southern sky.

Javier and José arrived with their lips set tightly together. Though they did not say anything, Patrick felt as if he should reassure them that whatever might come would not come that day, but he did not want to insinuate that they didn't trust him, so he said nothing. The three men set to work in terse silence, none of them showing any hint of panic or anxiety, but each with an awareness that the landscape upon which they stood might soon be a thing completely altered, might turn on them like a dog gone bad.

They worked, not rushed, but without the usual lulls and spaces of a normal workday. As the day passed, the light breeze of the early morning stiffened steadily. By mid-afternoon, the work was done. The anchors were set and the cable tied tightly around the structure. There was no planking yet, the dock still comprised only of pilings strung together with joists. But the planking would add buoyancy, and buoyancy was exactly what the dock would not need if a storm surge swelled underneath. Patrick would hold off until the storm passed.

When they finished packing up for the day, he stood in the yard and looked the dock up and down, and decided it was as sound as he could make it. He peered out at the marsh beyond the waterway, at the houses farther out that stood in rows near the beach, at the sky beyond the houses that spread out over open water. He tried to envision the thing that might be coming his way, tried to guess which direction it might take. He pictured how high the water might be at both high and low tides with a five-foot storm surge, ten feet, twenty feet. He figured the creek offered some protection; the water wasn't as fast-moving there as it was in the waterway. The island and the marsh might provide a buffer. All in all, he gave the fledgling dock a better than average chance of surviving if the hurricane made landfall nearby.

"We've done what we can," he said. "Get home, get yourselves squared away. Don't come back to work until this storm is gone, okay?

No work until after it's over. Do you understand?"

Javier nodded and translated to José, who nodded as well.

"Get home, stay home. Don't be driving around out there if this thing comes near us, okay?"

"Okay, boss," said Javier with a smile. "Don't worry about us. We'll be okay."

On his drive home, Patrick saw only a few people still lingering in town. In stark contrast to the early morning crowd, the public docks were all but abandoned. Most of the shops had closed early and a substantial portion of the town had already left in search of higher ground and inland relatives and friends. Those who remained in town were undoubtedly at home, busy securing their houses as best they could.

When Patrick got home, he went out on his own dock and dragged his boat out of the water and onto the mud flats. He sank the boat's anchor into the mud and tied a line from the boat to one of the pilings. Then he unscrewed the clamps on the outboard and muscled it off the boat. He carried it to his shed, then did the same with the chairs on the screened-in porch. He took the screen door from the porch off its hinges and stowed it under the deck. Experience had taught him that in a strong wind, the screen door tended to pull the latch out of the door frame and cause an unbelievable racket. When he was done, he took a look around the backyard and walked the perimeter of the house. Satisfied that all loose objects were as secure as he could make them, he went inside to check the forecast.

The television showed the typical weatherman in a raincoat near a bulkhead on some shore somewhere shouting over the wind as he gestured toward blowing trees and crashing waves. Eventually, the station switched to more useful information and showed a map of Anthony's progress as it inched along the coast. During the day, it had stayed offshore and continued northward until it stood in its current position off the coast of Georgia.

"Dammit," said Patrick to the television screen. "This thing just won't die."

The experts speculated that a strong westerly system would push the hurricane farther out to sea, where it would break apart at some point during the night. Patrick, however, had the growing suspicion that Anthony was not going to behave at all how an early-season storm is supposed to behave. It had already survived longer than it should have. He doubted it would be dissuaded by either westerly winds or cooler water temperatures.

He awoke to a flat, gray, looming sky that seemed to hang lower than usual. Occasional gusts of wind rattled the windows and sang through the screens on the back porch.

The waterway was choppy, and he wondered what the waves at the beach must look like if the normally calm waterway was so disturbed.

He turned on the television. The hurricane's progress was on the national news and all local stations had alert messages scrolling along the bottom of the screen. Anthony was off the coast of South Carolina and coming hard up the coast. It had not been pushed out to sea. It was going to have to grind to a halt over land, which meant that some people somewhere were going to have to pay a heavy price to stop it.

The storm was, however, starting to grow a little less tightly-wound at the center and wind speeds had dropped off somewhat. It was still a hurricane but just barely as its strength hovered between hurricane and tropical storm. But it was still large, dangerous, and headed on an uncertain bearing.

The meteorologists were hesitant to offer further conjecture. Patrick's hunch was that Anthony would move erratically as it began to come apart. Had it been later in the season, the warm water along the east coast could have led it past them as far north as New England. In the early season, however, the waters weren't warm yet and there was only so far the storm was likely to go before it weakened, lost its center, and spread out into an anticlimactic rainstorm.

A voluntary evacuation order was already in place for Watchman's Island. All residents were told in no uncertain terms that if they chose to stay, emergency services would not be available until after the storm had passed and rescue personnel could get to them safely. The bridge would be closed when the storm came near the island. The town of Spring Tide was on the mainland and would likely not be evacuated, but residents of towns up and down the coast had been cautioned not to drive unnecessarily until the storm had passed. The entire coast of North Carolina from the South Carolina border to the Outer Banks was hunkered down.

There was nothing left to do but wait.

By noon, it had grown so dark that it looked like sundown. The sky was marbled gray and the flat, ragged clouds looked bruised. The wind was constantly audible as it whipped through trees and slapped at window screens. Patrick could see whitecaps forming in the waterway and watched as the tide, pushed ahead by the winds, smacked against pilings and splashed onto the dock.

By mid afternoon, Patrick had lost his television signal, no doubt the result of one of the numerous branches and trees knocked down by the coming storm. The house began to creak under the strain of the wind. Leaves flew across the yard and small branches and bits of trash and debris cartwheeled down the street.

At some point in the late afternoon, the power went out and Patrick was left with no diversions, nothing to distract him from the siege that seemed to press in from all sides. The dog whimpered at Patrick's feet. The cat sought refuge under a bed and refused to come out. The house was now emitting a constant groan as the walls bore the strain of the unrelenting wind. Periodically, a sharp, screeching sound screamed above the din. It started at one end of the roof and spread across to the other side, and each time it happened, Patrick was sure the roof was coming off. The house, however, withstood the strain.

Night fell on an already darkened sky. Without electricity, he could not tell exactly where the storm was or when it would make landfall, but he knew it would be soon and that it would be close. The winds were too strong to be a mere glancing blow. Still, he was relieved that the storm had at least started to weaken. A stronger hurricane might have been more than his house could outlast.

He stretched out on the couch and tried to settle in for what promised to be at best a fitful night's rest. He nodded off a few times, but every time he closed his eyes, something outside made a loud crack or some bit of debris thumped into the side of the house and woke him up. Then his phone rang.

He was surprised that there was still phone service, and it took him a moment to pinpoint what the sound was. He fumbled for the phone in the dark.

"Hello, Mr. O'Reilly? Patrick?" came a voice on the other end, fighting to be heard above the background wind.

"Yes?" said Patrick.

"Is this Patrick?" asked the voice.

"Yes," said Patrick, louder.

"This is Doug Castin. Can you hear me?"

"I can hear you. What's wrong?"

"We can't find your dad," said Doug.

Patrick glanced at the churning darkness outside his living room window.

"Say that again?"

"We can't find your father. We don't know where he is."

"Jesus Christ, Doug. Where is he supposed to be? Are you at his house?"

"Yes sir," said Doug. "I got here just a few minutes ago and he's not here. His car is gone."

"Where's the staff?"

"I don't know, sir. Mr. O'Reilly must have dismissed them to tend to their families."

"What the hell, Doug? Was he left there by himself in a goddamn hurricane? Was someone supposed to be watching him?"

There was a pause. Patrick could hear only wind.

"Answer me, Doug. Who's supposed to be there?"

"Your brother Sean. I . . . we don't know where he is either. I guess he left town."

Patrick pulled the phone away from his ear and cursed. He swung his fist down onto the counter hard enough to make a spoon jump out of an empty bowl.

"Where's Jack?" asked Patrick.

"He's on his way here."

"Damn, Doug. You guys shouldn't be driving around in this shit."

"We think your father might be trying to get to your house," said Doug.

"My house? Why in hell would he be coming here? He hasn't been here in years."

"Yesterday he said something to Mr. Kent and me. He wasn't very coherent. He kept saying something about the island, and he said your name. We didn't think anything of it until now."

"I'm not on the island. That doesn't make any sense. Doug, is this your best lead? You think he's driving through a hurricane to come see *me*?"

There was no response.

"Where's Bryan? Could Dad be headed over there?"

"He's at home. Alone. He wasn't answering his phone so Mr. Kent went over there first. Bryan hasn't spoken to your father recently. He hasn't seen him."

"Well, my father's not here. And there are trees down everywhere. If he is on his way, he'll never make it."

"Should I go search for him? When Mr. Kent arrives, he could wait here in case your father returns."

"No, stay put. There's no point trying to drive around out there if you don't have any idea where you're going. You'll get yourself killed. Let's just try to remember anything else he might have said, okay? Any location at all, any place. Did he mention anything other than the island?"

"No. The only conversation I've had with your father in the past week was the one I already mentioned."

"What did he say about the island? You said he kept talking about it."

"He did, sir. It didn't make much sense. We were watching the weather forecast and he kept talking about the island, about the hurricane. He wasn't speaking in complete sentences."

A thought occurred to Patrick, a long shot.

"Did he mention the hurricane by name? Did he say the word 'Anthony'?"

"I don't believe so."

"You said he said my name. Did he say my full name?"

"Yes sir. He said 'Patrick O'Reilly.' He said it pointedly; he was looking me in the eyes."

"Like he was addressing you or like he was relaying information to you?" asked Patrick.

"I did not get the impression that he thought I was you, if that's what you mean. He was speaking as if he wanted me to remember the name. He was enunciating very carefully."

Patrick O'Reilly.

Padraig O'Reilly.

"Oh my God," said Patrick. "Have they closed the bridge?"

"Beg your pardon?"

"Have they closed the bridge yet? The bridge to the island. Is it closed?"

"I'm not sure. I haven't heard anything."

"Well, I'll have to check," said Patrick. "It's the only place I can think of."

"Surely you don't intend to try to drive out to the island?"

"He's not here and he's not there. Do you have any other ideas?" asked Patrick. "He's out there somewhere and that's my only idea."

"Then I'm coming with you."

"No, you're not. There's no sense in both of us being out there. You stay put in case he comes home. Wait for Jack."

"It's too dangerous, Patrick. It's suicide. You'll—"

Patrick hung up the phone before Doug could protest further. He snatched his keys off the counter, took a deep breath, and opened the door. As soon as he stepped outside, the wind struck him so hard he could not breathe. He turned his back to the wind, felt the back of his neck tingle and his hands go weak. He hesitated, then ducked his head back into the house.

The dog, which had followed him to the kitchen, eyed the outside warily, shifted his weight from paw to paw, pressed his ears flat.

"Come on, Neptune. Come on, boy."

Neptune eased out the door, pressed his weight against Patrick's leg. Patrick scratched under the dog's chin and fought the door closed behind him. He tucked his chin to his chest, took a deep breath in the lee his body created, and led Neptune to the Jeep.

The night sky streaked by at an unsettling rate; the clouds moved so fast that when Patrick fixated on the sky for more than a glance, it made him dizzy. He drove slowly down his darkened street and through the deserted town, picking his way through the branches and debris that snapped and crunched underneath the tires. He passed a downed power line that writhed and twitched like a decapitated snake. The wind was a low, rasping howl that tore at the sides of the Jeep so fiercely the wheel shook in Patrick's hands and he had to fight to avoid being pushed sideways off the road.

He was alone on the highway. Traffic lights danced in jarring discombobulation. Trees were bowed and flailing and distorted into the shape of inside-out umbrellas. The highway was less cluttered with branches than were the neighborhood roads. The wind, however, was unbroken out in the open and it blew so loudly that even the sound of the Jeep's engine was drowned out.

He turned onto the road to the bridge. Rain began to pelt his windshield, large, round drops that hit with solid force. A foreboding sense of enclosure and isolation overcame Patrick, as if the inside of the vehicle was a tiny air bubble suspended within a vast body of water, the wind and rain a single undifferentiated mass that pressed against the minute protected space from all sides. An awareness of being small clung to him as he pushed on through the unending, unyielding black. He was glad he had brought the dog.

His whole world was the road ahead illuminated by headlights and smeared by rain, and it was by the most fickle thread of fate that he even saw it at all. Close to the bridge, down the slope and nearly under one of the embankments. A light, a flickering and faded light that caught the outermost edge of Patrick's vision, the only bit of light at all outside the periphery of his own headlights.

He stopped and stared, trying to make out what it was, trying to draw some shape around it. The rain made it impossible. He tried to inch closer to the side of the road but did not want to get too close, afraid the wind would push the Jeep over and send it rolling down the slope. Neptune grew uneasy, whimpered, pawed at Patrick's arm. He considered moving on, leaving the mystery unsolved, but he could not.

He fought the door open and stepped out onto the road. He had to crouch against the wind. The sideways-streaking rain stung his face. He squinted at the light and took a few cautious steps down the slope, Neptune close at his heels, tail tucked between his legs. The darkened outline of a car emerged from the gloom. It was at rest inches from the rising waterway. Only a concrete support that jutted out from the bridge had stopped it from disappearing into the water.

Patrick continued down the slope, half walking and half sliding, until he came to the narrow bank. He inched closer to the car. The front end was smashed. One headlight was out, the other, splashed with mud, emitted only a frail beam that shone weakly through the driving rain. He approached the car with caution, not sure what or whom he might find. It was an expensive sedan; he could tell by the shape. It was a dark color, but in the minimal light he couldn't make out the shade. He searched his memory for his father's car but no image presented itself.

He moved within arm's reach but still could not see through the windows. He worked his way around to the driver's side door and was within reach of the door handle when Neptune stiffened at his side. The dog's fear dissolved in an instant. He growled into the dark, ears upright and pointed toward the water. Patrick followed the dog's stare, saw nothing, then movement. A figure, not twenty yards away, was staggering along the bank towards him.

Patrick's chest tightened and the breath caught in his throat. He held onto Neptune's collar and leaned into the wind, tried to identify the person approaching from the maelstrom. The figure's hair, blown wild by the storm, was a scattered blur of white. He stood rigid amidst the scouring wind and made no effort to shield himself from the rain. The effect was ethereal, spectral, as if the man were an apparition emerging from spray blown from the crests of the white-capped peaks thrashing through the waterway behind him.

The man was muttering something as he came, but Patrick could not make out the words. He took a few tentative steps and recognized his father's face in the scant light of the lone working headlight. As he drew closer, he saw a deep cut above his father's eyebrow. Rain-diluted blood streaked Henry's face and stained the collar of his shirt. His eyebrows were raised and his eyes wide as they darted wildly between the car and Patrick.

"What happened here?" his father asked.

"Dad, is this your car? You've been in an accident," Patrick said.

He took his shirt off and pressed it against the cut on his father's head. Henry tried to jerk away from his son's hand but Patrick reached his free arm around his father's back and held him in place.

"It's not safe out here," said Patrick. "We need to get you home."

"What is this? What are you doing here?" asked his father as he managed to twist free.

"Dad, it's not safe. We need to go. Come on," said Patrick. He took his father's arm to guide him up the slope but Henry pulled away.

"Do you know who I am?" asked Patrick, on a hunch.

His father looked up at him, studied his face for a moment, his brow wrinkled.

"Of course I do. Now let's get moving. We have to get over there."

Patrick knew that he was lying, that he had guessed that Patrick was someone he should have recognized. There had been no recognition in either his face or his voice. And Patrick had heard his father lie before. He was familiar with the sound.

"We need to get over there," said Henry again, more urgently. "We can't wait. There isn't time. We need to get over there." He pointed into the howling abyss in the general direction of the island.

"Time for what? Why?" asked Patrick as he cast a wary eye at the bridge that loomed above them.

"We need to get over there," said Henry, his voice growing stronger. "We need to get over there *now*."

"I don't understand. What's over there? Why do you need to get over there?"

"He's over there. He's on the island and we need to get to him. There isn't time."

His father's eyes darted sideways as if he were a spooked horse. He searched the darkness beyond the bridge, scanning in vain for some mystery point on the island. Patrick gripped his father's lapels with both hands and pulled him close to him until he could see into his father's eyes. He saw raw panic and sheer desperation, he saw shock, but he did not see comprehension. He could not find his father anywhere in the wide, bloodshot orbs that stared back at him.

"There isn't time," said his father, his voice sagging to not much more than a hoarse whimper. "There isn't time. We have to go. There isn't time."

"Who's over there?" asked Patrick. "Who are you trying to find? Who's over there?"

"O'Reilly. Padraig O'Reilly is his name. He's over there and we need to go and get him."

Patrick knew that they were standing in two different storms. Henry was trying to rescue his father, dead for more than thirty years. He had driven through a hurricane to mend an ancient past he could not escape.

"It's not safe out here," said Patrick. "Let's get you out of here. Come on."

He took his father's arm and tried to guide him up the slope to the road but his father still would not go. He was staring back at the smashed car.

"Come on, Dad. We'll come back for the car. It's not safe," said Patrick, but again his father did not move. His head was cocked to one side as if he had just stumbled upon the car and couldn't figure out how it had gotten there. Patrick followed his father's gaze but did not see anything other than the lone headlight and the dark shape. And then a sinking sensation swept through him.

"Is someone still in there?"

Henry looked at Patrick with open-mouthed incomprehension.

"Dad, did someone come here with you? Is there someone in the car?"

"Why are you here?" asked Henry.

"Stay right here, okay?" said Patrick.

He returned to the car and felt his way around it until he got to the passenger side. He felt for the door but it was locked. He cupped his hands on the window and looked in and at first saw only colors, incongruous white and red in an otherwise gray and black night. He scrambled around to the driver's side and threw open the door. As soon as he did, Neptune barked a sharp warning and tried to push past him.

"Easy," said Patrick. "Easy." He was not sure whether he was talking to the dog or to himself. He nudged the dog aside and climbed into the car.

She was slumped against the window, her head resting at an unnatural angle against the passenger-side window. Her face was obscured by her limp, blood-soaked white hair. Blood was smeared on the window of the car door; blood had pooled in her lap.

Patrick noticed odd, inconsequential things. A diamond earring poked through the bloody hair. The fingernails on her visible hand were dark red and newly painted. A gold chain fell against her collar and glittered in the meager light.

He took a deep breath and exhaled, slow and tattered, then leaned forward and checked for a pulse. There was none. He put a hand in front of her mouth but felt no breath, no warmth at all. He touched her face and her hands, which were cold and rigid.

Marie Bouchard was dead.

CHAPTER SEVENTEEN

Patrick stared transfixed at the lifeless form with which he shared the confined space, consumed with how artificial she looked in death. He exhaled suddenly, violently; he had not realized he had been holding his breath. He could hear his heartbeat in his ears.

He felt movement behind him and shook his head to regain focus. He backed out of the car and used his body to block his father from peering inside. Something about Henry triggered Neptune's protective instinct and the dog stood alongside as if to keep the man upright. Henry kept a hand on the dog's shoulder, the two beings coevolved to lean and be leaned upon.

"Let's get going, Dad," said Patrick. "Come on."

He put an arm around his father's shoulders and turned him away from the car but his father pulled away suddenly and Patrick lost his footing in the mud.

"Do not open that door!" Patrick shouted, too late. Before he could get to his feet, his father had climbed into the driver's side and shut the door behind him. A desperate, forlorn howl, muted only slightly by the enclosed car, tore through the night.

Patrick opened the door and saw his father staring at Marie. His mouth worked furiously but only a strangled gasp came out. Patrick put his hands underneath his father's armpits and eased him out of the car. His father did not resist. All the fight had left him.

Patrick stood his father up, but each time he withdrew his support, his father slumped towards the ground and he had to catch him. He wrapped an arm around his father's chest and dragged him backwards up the slope. He muscled him into the Jeep and closed the door, let Neptune into the back, and climbed behind the wheel. He started the engine but did not leave. He looked at the bridge that led to his father's past. He looked down the slope at the lone light still glimmering in the driving rain. Then he made a choice.

He hurried down the slope and crawled into the driver's side of the smashed car. With a whispered apology to Marie, he unbuckled her seatbelt. He wrestled down his doubt and revulsion, and the shame he felt at his own action and, putting his arms around Marie's waist, dragged her from the passenger side of the car to the driver's side. Her head lolled as she was moved, hit with a sickly, empty thud against the side window. Her hair brushed against Patrick's cheek as he swung her feet over and buckled the seatbelt around her. He went around to the passenger side and wiped the blood off the windows with his shirt. When he was done, he made a quick examination of the car, then closed the door. He checked the rising waterway. It was already up to the tires and swirling around his ankles.

The water would continue to rise. He knew it would rise; he knew the tides, like musicians, know time. The tide would continue to come in and, with the aid of the wind and the storm surge that was sending Anthony to its death on the shore, it would rise enough to swallow the car, to bathe it and cleanse it of any remaining evidence of what he had done.

He rinsed his hands in the waterway and climbed back up the slope. He was afraid his father would object as he turned the car around and drove away from the bridge, but Henry's mouth only hung open as he stared vacantly at some point in the infinite distance. The bridge and the island, the entire misbegotten quest, were abandoned dreams.

Patrick could think of nothing to say to him.

Jack was waiting for them when they arrived at Patrick's house. He helped Henry out of the car and into the house. Once safely inside, Jack looked to Patrick for an explanation. Patrick shook his head. Jack watched him for a long moment.

"Here, Henry, take these," said Jack. He handed Henry two white pills.

Henry looked solemnly at Jack, at the pills in his hand.

"They'll help you sleep," said Jack.

Henry's lips moved and he said something to Jack but it came out only as a dry crackling sound. He swallowed the pills.

"Is that your blood?" asked Jack, pointing at Patrick.

"No."

"Do you think he needs any medical treatment? He's got a pretty good cut on his head there."

"I don't think so," said Patrick. "He was coherent. Well, more or less."

Jack wiped Henry's face clean with a towel, then dressed and bandaged the wound. Patrick could hear Jack breathing through his nose while he worked. Jack's mouth was a straight line. When he was done, he turned to Patrick.

"Can he stay here tonight? He looks pretty worn out and I don't want to risk taking him back out there."

"Of course," said Patrick.

The two men helped Henry into Patrick's bedroom. They undressed him and put him in the bed. The medication took effect and Henry fell asleep. They left the room and Jack closed the door behind them.

"He was over by the bridge," said Patrick once they were back in the kitchen. "He wrecked his car."

"What was he doing there?"

"He thought it was Hurricane Francesca. He was reliving it. He thought he was on his way to rescue his father. I guess the storm triggered the memory and he didn't . . . I guess he didn't remember what year it was."

Jack nodded slowly. His eyes did not leave Patrick's face. Patrick could feel Jack looking at him but could not lift his head.

"What else?" asked Jack.

"Marie was in the car," said Patrick. "She's dead."

"Say that again?"

"Marie's dead, Jack. She died in the accident."

Jack exhaled loudly and put a thumb to his mouth.

"Did you leave her there?"

Patrick nodded.

"And you're sure she's dead? You're positive?"

Patrick nodded again.

"Well, this is a whole different matter now," said Jack. "We need to contact the police. We'll need to explain this somehow. This is not good."

"We don't need to call the police," said Patrick. "I've taken care of it."

"What do you mean by that?"

Patrick tried to swallow the lump in his throat.

"Jack, I did something out there and I swear I don't know if it was the right thing or not."

"What was it? What did you do, Patty?"

"I moved her. I moved the body."

"Where did you move her?"

"I found her in the passenger seat. I moved her to the driver's side. I knew they'd investigate and I wasn't sure . . . I didn't know if it was a good idea for the whole town to know my father had driven around in the middle of a hurricane and accidentally killed his fiancée. He can get away with a lot, but this might be too much."

"And you don't want everyone to know that your father is sick," said Jack.

Patrick shrugged.

"Of course," Patrick said. "But now all anyone will remember about Marie is that she was a crazy woman who drove off in a hurricane and got herself killed. Hell, my guess is that she was only trying to help. I'm sure Dad wasn't making much sense. She probably went with him just to look after him. And look what happened."

Patrick rubbed his temples with the thumb and middle finger of his hand.

"That's Marie's blood on you? Or your father's?" asked Jack.

"Little of both, I guess."

"Give that shirt to me. I'll get rid of it."

Patrick handed it to Jack.

"You did the right thing, Patty. You were protecting this town and you did right by your father. It's a shame about Marie and we'll do what we can. But that body belongs to Sean," said Jack with icy finality.

"You spoke to Doug?"

"Of course. The only reason Doug left your father's house to begin with was that Sean specifically told him to do so. Sean sent him home with his assurance that he'd remain at the house for the duration of the storm."

"Do you think Sean left on purpose? Do you think he meant for Dad to hurt himself?" asked Patrick.

"I doubt it. It was probably carelessness. Or he may have just been scared of the storm. But it doesn't much matter now, does it?"

"I don't know. I guess not. He's either a coward or a murderer. He's a son of a bitch either way," said Patrick.

"I should go. I have some loose ends to tie up," said Jack.

"No way," said Patrick. "It's too nasty out there."

"It's dying down a little. The worst is over, at any rate."

"You're sure? There's plenty of room here if you need to stay."

"You'll call me when he wakes up?"

Patrick nodded. Jack gripped Patrick's shoulder and left. When he was gone, Patrick went to the window at the rear of the house and looked out at what was left of Anthony, now not much more than a heavy rain. He wondered when the rescue personnel would resume their work, when some cop would notice the car down on the bank underneath the bridge. He wondered if the last headlight of his father's car had burned out yet, if the water had risen high enough to short out the battery, or if perhaps the light was underwater but still aglow, a tiny bright spot in a black and murky world, a final luminescent rebellion against the blank sameness of all things covered by dark water.

Patrick showered and lay down on the couch and tried to convince himself to sleep, but he could not and was not surprised.

Every time he closed his eyes, he saw her face. As the night drew towards its end and he grew sleepier, the face became increasingly grotesque. It lost its skin, became a bare skull with her hair, became a skull that could talk, became a skull that had real eyes that stared back at him. As the first hint of dawn crept along the horizon, the face regained its human form, asking silent questions from out of its shattered and bloody visage. Its final incarnation was a healthy undamaged version, the one Patrick had seen the last time he had spoken to her, except she was not smiling.

Once the sun had risen and shone in oblique streaks through the blinds, Patrick gave up on sleep and stepped outside into the brightness. The view had altered as quickly and dramatically as a set change in a play. The waterway was flat and calm except for the faintest trace of a ripple blown across the surface by a warm, lazy breeze. A few wisps of white clouds floated through a benign sky. It was as if the weather was making an apology for its outburst; only the downed tree limbs and strewn debris revealed any trace of the previous night's tantrum.

He heard motion from inside the house. He went back inside and knocked cautiously on the bedroom door. Footsteps approached, then the door opened a crack. A solitary eye showed through the opening. It looked Patrick up and down.

"Why are you here? Where am I?" asked his father.

"You're at my house, Dad. I'm your son Patrick."

"Jesus Christ, I know full well who you are, Patty. What the hell's wrong with you?"

"You just asked me where you were. How was I supposed to know you knew who I was?"

His father opened the door wide.

"I was asking where I was because I didn't recognize whose house I was in. How the hell am I supposed to know what the inside of your little shack looks like?"

Patrick stared dumbstruck.

"Where's your mother?" continued Henry belligerently.

Patrick was not sure how to proceed. He said nothing.

"Don't just stand there with your mouth open, boy. Answer me."

"My mother? I . . . she's not . . . she passed away, Dad."

Henry's eyes narrowed and he leaned forward.

"Well, of course she did, idiot boy. I meant Marie, not your mother. I misspoke. Jesus Christ," he said.

"Do you . . . what do you remember about last night?" asked Patrick.

Henry made an irritated, impatient circular motion with his hand.

"Come on, come on. I've got work to do today, Patty. I don't have time to rehash my whole life for you. Now refresh my memory. Why am I here again?"

"I think maybe we should call Jack," said Patrick.

"Sure. Fine. Let's get someone in here who knows what they're doing. Let's get someone over here who can answer a goddamn question."

Patrick went into the kitchen and called Jack, who informed him that he was already on the way over.

"Can't get here soon enough," said Patrick as he hung up the phone.

"What was that?" demanded his father from the living room.

"Nothing," said Patrick. "He'll be here in a few minutes."

Henry took a seat in a chair in the living room. Patrick sat on the couch and looked apprehensively at his father. His father rubbed his hands on his knees impatiently.

"You know, right?" asked Patrick. "You know about your . . . about the condition you have?"

"What condition?"

"They told you, right? The doctors?"

His father leaned in towards him.

"What I do and don't know is none of your goddamn business, son. I thought you made it damn clear that you don't want any part of the business."

"What does this have to do with the business?"

"Plenty, that's what," said Henry.

Patrick held up his hands in surrender.

"You know what, Dad? You're kind of a son of a bitch. It's no wonder Sean's a son of a bitch too."

Henry's face grew a dangerous shade of red but a knock on the door staved off a response. Patrick let Jack in.

"Do you have my car, Jack?" asked Henry as he rose from his chair.

"No. We'll take mine."

"Fine," said Henry, and without further ado swept past both Patrick and Jack and out the door.

"Are you coming with us?" asked Jack. "We're going back to his house."

"Hell, no. I don't need the aggravation," said Patrick. "He was so out of it. Now he's the same as he's always been but doesn't remember anything about last night."

"His memory comes and goes," said Jack. "For whatever reason, it's usually best in the morning."

"So you're not going to tell him that he killed his fiancée?"

"He knows. He just doesn't remember right now. It's in there somewhere."

"But he won't acknowledge anything."

"He's covering. He knows enough to know that he forgets things. He's smart enough most of the time to make educated guesses about who he knows or what he does. If he doesn't recall something, he generally gets by with brusqueness. Or outright rudeness."

"But what happens if he suddenly remembers everything from last night? It'll ruin him. Hell, maybe not. Maybe he doesn't give a damn."

"He won't trust his brain enough to believe it if he does remember. That should cushion the blow. That's my guess, anyway. Nobody really seems to know anything for sure about this disease."

"Any word about the car?"

"The police found her last night. They didn't ask any questions that led me to believe they were interested in pursuing the matter as anything more than an accident."

"They didn't think it was odd that Marie drove my father's car into a bridge in the middle of a hurricane?"

"They did. But you know how things go in this town. As long as they're not forced to notice something, they'll make every effort not to."

"So Marie just looks like some unbalanced woman who got herself killed," said Patrick.

"I should go, Patty. He'll get impatient. We're looking for Sean. When we find him, we're all going to get together and try to come up with some answers about what happened last night. You should be there."

"Fine," Patrick said.

Jack closed the door behind him. Patrick watched through the window as Jack got into his car. He could see their faces. Neither Jack nor Henry spoke as they backed out of the driveway.

CHAPTER EIGHTEEN

A trawler had sunk along the town wharf. People were gathered around the foundered boat as if it were a coffin. They helplessly stared down at the unnatural angle of the outriggers that protruded from the water. A big man with a shaggy white beard whom Patrick did not recognize was wiping tears from red-rimmed eyes.

Elsewhere throughout the town, tree limbs and a few entire trees were down. The roof of a porch had collapsed on one of the houses across the road from the docks. A convenience store had a display window shattered and the owner was sweeping up the glass. A traffic light had come crashing down and its wreckage pulled off to the side of the road. No one was directing traffic at the intersection, but Patrick was more or less alone on the roads. Most people had either left ahead of the storm or were busy cleaning up after it.

Sean had resurfaced without apology. Patrick was on his way to meet with him and Jack and whoever else had been asked to come. On his way, however, he decided to stop by the Macready place to see to what extent his work had been destroyed.

Trepidation writhed in his stomach as he made the turn onto Mr. Macready's street. He was not sure what he would do if the dock was a complete loss. Neither he nor Mr. Macready could afford to start over from the beginning.

He was relieved, however, to find it mostly intact. One of the pilings towards the end of the dock had been pushed sideways by wind and water and would have to be replaced. A few of the joists had also pulled free, but overall no more than a few days' work had been lost. A line had snapped on the barge but they had tied extras and it was still secure. Patrick climbed aboard and cut the old line free so that it wouldn't foul the props. He coiled the line and put it away in a locker. He went to inspect the crane for damage and nearly stepped on Javier, who was lying underneath a tarp on the deck.

Patrick knelt next to him and put a hand on his shoulder, not yet sure whether he was dead or sleeping. Javier's arm jerked, his eyes flew open, and Patrick sighed in relief. Javier shielded his eyes from the intrusive light and offered a sheepish grin.

"Sorry, Boss," he said. "Sorry to sleep here."

"What the hell are you doing here, Javier? Did you stay here last night?"

"Sí. Yes. I stay last night in the storm but I fall asleep in the morning. Sorry."

"Jesus, Javier, you could have been killed. Why on earth did you stay here? You should have called me if you needed a place to stay."

Javier laughed.

"No, no, no, it's not like that," he said. "I have a place. I stay here to make sure nothing bad happens."

"What are you saying? You spent the night on the barge just to look after it?" asked Patrick.

Javier nodded.

"Yes. Of course. No barge, no work."

"Sure, but . . . Javier, you could have died out here."

Javier shrugged. Patrick scratched his head and looked incredulously around the barge.

"Where did you stay when it got bad? There's nowhere to get out of the weather on this thing."

Javier pointed to the crane on the foredeck.

"I sit where you sit. In there."

"In the cabin? Of the crane?"

Javier nodded.

"Shit, man. What if that crane had blown over? What if it had fallen overboard with you inside it?"

"It's okay. It didn't blow over."

Patrick shook his head. "Javier, you're a damn good man. You know that?"

Javier shrugged and smiled. "No barge, no work," he repeated.

"As long as I've got work, you've got work. Okay?" said Patrick. "Now, let's get you the hell off this boat. Do you need a ride?"

"José will come when I call him," he said.

Patrick walked with Javier back to the yard and waited with him until José pulled up. Patrick thanked him again and the two men drove off. Then he turned back to the water, to the serene, glittering green creek, and he tried to imagine what it must have looked like a few hours earlier from inside the tiny cabin of the crane with a hurricane hurling everything it had left directly at him.

The image of Javier alone in the storm would not leave him as he drove. The fact that Javier had assumed incorrectly that destruction of their equipment meant the loss of his job did not diminish Patrick's overwhelming appreciation for the risk Javier had taken, the fear he must have endured. He was staggered by the act, even if it was not entirely selfless.

The same storm that would not likely have been life-threatening to Sean could easily have killed Javier. The idea festered. The disparity between the two men was too much for Patrick to reconcile. As he pulled into the parking lot of Coastal Seafood headquarters, he took several deep breaths to try to relieve the pressure in his chest, but it did not work.

There were only a few cars. With streets still littered with debris and several neighborhoods still without power, the staff had been given the day off to tend to their homes and families. Jack was waiting for him outside the entrance.

"I thought you were banned from the building," said Patrick as he got out of the car.

"I was," said Jack.

"And yet here you are," said Patrick. "Did Sean invite you? Is he planning some kind of massacre?"

"He isn't aware that I'm here. He's under the impression that your father asked to meet with him."

Patrick frowned. "Are *you* planning a massacre?"

Jack smiled. "Something like that."

"Well, whatever he gets will be too good for him," said Patrick. "Are we waiting for someone else?"

Jack scanned the parking lot and the street behind. "I suppose not," he said.

Once inside the building, Patrick followed Jack to the same meeting room in which Jack had been fired. Only Sean and Helen were in the room, seated next to each other.

"Nice," said Patrick. "Don't even bother hiding it."

Sean ignored him. Helen looked sour.

"What are you doing here? Where is my father?" Sean said to Jack.

"He couldn't make it. I'm here on his behalf," said Jack.

Sean opened his mouth to speak but opted to feign indifference instead.

"Where is Bryan?" Jack asked Helen.

"He couldn't make it," said Helen. "I came instead."

Something that looked like doubt creased Jack's brow. In an instant, it was gone.

"And you two have discussed the matter? You are aware of why we're here today?"

A look of contemptuous confidence swept across Helen's sharp-featured face.

"What my husband and I have discussed is none of your affair," she said.

"Look, Jack," interjected Sean, "you're lucky we even let you in here. Quit wasting my time and get on with it."

"Very well," said Jack.

He took a seat across the table from Sean and Helen, gestured toward an empty chair for Patrick. Jack's every motion, every slight action, radiated poise and control, as if each movement had been practiced until flawless and sharp.

"Your actions over the past forty-eight hours have been deplorable," said Jack, addressing Sean.

Patrick felt the abruptness of the words. A muscle in his neck twitched. The room sat quiet for a long quiet moment as if a great noise were still reverberating within it.

Sean met Jack's gaze but couldn't hold it. He snorted, then forced out an unnatural sounding laugh.

"Is that a fact?" he said.

"Do you deny that it was your responsibility to tend to your father last night?"

"Must have been a mix-up. My assistant dropped the ball. He's completely useless."

"Did you or did you not leave your father unattended during the storm?"

"I don't deny anything. I told you. It was Dougie's fault. You want me to fire him for it? I'll fire him. Doesn't mean shit to me."

"You're a fucking liar," said Patrick under his breath.

"What was that?" asked Sean.

Jack held a hand up toward Patrick but did not take his eyes off Sean.

"Never mind that," Jack said. "I'm trying to make sure that we are all in agreement about the facts. I'd like to be certain of the chain of events so we're not making any unjust accusations. That said, I quite agree with Patrick. I believe you are lying," said Jack.

He spoke the words as if he were inserting a knife. The room seemed to grow colder. The tension shrank the space and Jack and Sean appeared closer to each other than they were.

Sean leaned forward in his chair.

"It's a goddamn shame you feel that way, Jack. It's also a goddamn shame that I don't answer to you, and I do what I please, when I please. If, for example, I want to get out of town rather than sit through a hurricane, then that's what I'm going to damn well do."

Patrick jumped to his feet with such ferocity that his chair toppled over backwards.

"A person is *dead*, you son of a bitch!" he roared down at Sean. "You don't give a shit? Well, good for you. But a person is *dead*, for Christ's sake. Who's supposed to carry that? Who? Dad? Our dad who forgets his own name? Is he supposed to carry it?"

"Oh, stow it, Patty," said Sean. "No one's interested in your thoughts. Besides, I don't remember seeing you at Dad's place when I left, either. You were just as absent as I was."

Patrick slammed both hands on the table and heat radiated from his face, but no words would come. He was angry beyond his ability to control it, but his anger could not drown out the sinking feeling that Sean might not be wrong. The truth moved around him like air: guilt was contagious and they were all sick.

"I don't believe it makes a difference," said Jack. "Sean, you had agreed to be there and Patrick had not."

"Now listen here," said Sean, shaking a twitchy finger at Jack. "You've already been fired, but I can still make things a lot worse for you."

"Sean, the larger issue, and the only important one, is that you are no more fit to care for your father than you are to run the company," said Jack. "I believe that you've been granted too much power and that you have too little respect for that power. I intend to have it taken from you."

"You can't speak to me like that! You're in *my* building. I am in control here!"

"Are you?"

Sean's breath came in heaves, but he resisted. He sat back in his chair and threw his arms out wide.

"How are you going to take it from me? Sure, you sound convincing in a meeting. You carry yourself well. But you don't have any authority, do you? For all the reputation, for all the people in this backwards town that are so afraid of you, at the end of the day, you're just some unemployed asshole with a lot of opinions. You don't like how I run things? Fine. What can you do about it?"

"I intend to prove in a court of law that your father was not of sufficient cognitive health to make an informed decision when he signed the contract that endowed you with your shares of the company. Bryan," Jack glanced over at Helen, "was surprisingly accepting of the idea. I doubt he particularly enjoyed the ownership position."

"Now wait just a minute," said Helen, who had up to that point watched the conversation with detached interest. "Bryan can't forfeit his share. I won't allow it."

"He won't have to," said Jack. "A rising tide sinks all boats. The same lawsuit that will ultimately strip Sean of his ownership will also divest Bryan of his. And, of course, by extension you will also lose any claim of ownership in the company."

Helen's face turned white. She looked accusingly at Sean.

"And you're just going to allow this?" she snapped.

"We have plenty of lawyers. If it's a legal battle you want, we'll give all you can handle."

"Not to worry, Sean," said Jack. "You'll no doubt be taken care of. It isn't your father's goal to make you a pauper. And it would be bad for the company's image. However, I doubt you'll ever see a controlling interest again."

Sean's face, already red, began to turn purple. His chin quivered. The two parties remained seated with Jack on one side of the table, earnest and serene, and on the other Sean and Helen beginning to unravel. Patrick remained standing, his hands flat on the table's surface as if he were presiding over the meeting when in fact he was not quite sure of his role. He liked that Sean and Helen were agitated even if he wasn't sure what cards Jack held beyond his threat to sue.

Patrick heard something—a shuffle, a padded footstep; the generic, indistinct, barely audible sound of the energy of a human life—he wasn't sure what he heard. He wasn't even sure if the sensation was a sound at all. Later, he would wonder how he had missed someone walking into the room, how none of them had heard or seen the door open. He turned his head and saw Bryan standing behind his right shoulder, so close that Patrick recoiled from the disorienting shock of his appearance.

His face was sallow. Large black patches sagged below his eyes. He was wearing a wrinkled and untucked dress shirt stained yellow around the neck. His mouth hung down at an angle that made the bottom half of his face look twisted. The top half of his face, however, showed nothing but a vague sense of determination. He was staring past Patrick so intently that Patrick was not sure Bryan even saw him at all.

"You go ahead and try," said Sean from across the table.

Patrick assumed Sean was still talking to Jack, but when he turned back to the room, he saw that Bryan had finally been noticed by the others. Patrick did not understand Sean's words or the mockery in his voice. He turned back to Bryan for clarification and saw the gun wrapped inside a white-knuckled fist that hung limp by his side.

"Bryan—" said Patrick.

"I'm serious," said Sean. "You go ahead and try. You haven't got the guts."

"Enough, Sean," said Jack. "That's enough. Bryan, put that gun away."

"What for?" sneered Sean, rising to his feet. "I'll even give him a clear shot." He held his arms out to his sides.

As Sean smiled at Bryan, Patrick felt the hair on his neck stand on end. He was sure Sean was on comfortable ground. Bryan's intrusion was a welcome reprieve from Jack's relentless stare. But Patrick had looked into Bryan's eyes and seen none of the usual resignation.

"I don't think that's wise, Sean," said Jack.

"For the last time, no one gives a damn what you think, Jack. Now come on, Bryan, let's go. If you're not too much of a coward."

Stop it, Sean. You don't understand. You need to stop.

Bryan's arm moved mechanically upward and came to a stop with his elbow at a ninety-degree angle. Patrick was within arm's reach of the gun. He eyed it carefully. He was calculating whether he could snatch it out of his brother's hand when a flash shot from the barrel and a crack thundered through the small room, so loud that it sounded like it had gone off inside Patrick's skull.

Patrick jerked away from the sound and put his hands to his ears. He could hear nothing beyond the ringing. A bitter taste filled his mouth. He looked around the room but the images were murky and seemed to flicker as if he were looking at a series of photographs. He shook his head to clarify the images as he looked around the room.

He saw Sean covered in blood with flecks of something shiny and gray splattered across his face and chest. He saw Helen duck her head onto her arm on the table. A whitish-red cloud hung in the air over the two of them. Something dissonant made him look back at Helen and he saw that a section of the back of her head was missing and that she had not, in fact, put her head onto her arm to hide from the gunshot. He looked back at Sean and saw that only the whites of his eyes were not red. His hands were half-raised and shaking.

The gun fired again and a splash of red erupted from Sean's chest. Patrick turned as another shot fired. The hand holding the gun twitched and Patrick could see every feature of the pistol in immaculate detail as he reached wildly for it. He caught the gun and the hand that held it and it burned his palm, but he did not care.

Bryan looked at the gun and the hand that held it as if he were unsure whose hand it was. He tried to pull free but Patrick would not let go. They stood there for a long moment in their odd stalemate while Patrick, who had thought no further than trying to make the gun stop shooting, held the gun and its attached hand motionless. Bryan had the better angle and all the leverage but Patrick was much stronger and would not budge.

Bryan looked at him. Patrick saw Bryan's brow creased and his jaw set, but there was neither excitement nor regret nor fear, no tension and no joy and no relief and no panic, none of the things that Patrick expected to see.

"Please," said Bryan softly, as if he were making a rational request.

"Bryan, no."

"Patty, please," said Bryan. "Please, just let go. Let me finish this. Please just let me finish this."

Had the request not come from his own brother, it would have seemed patently absurd. It took Patrick a sluggish moment to come to the obvious conclusion that it was not a request he could honor.

"I'm sorry, Bryan," he said, and with a quick, snapping motion he jerked Bryan's hand, nearly dragging Bryan off his feet as he pulled him closer. He swung his left fist hard at Bryan's incoming jaw. His head snapped backwards and he collapsed onto the floor.

Patrick pried Bryan's fingers from the gun and held it in his palm. It was the first gun he had ever held. He was surprised how heavy it felt.

"Patrick!" yelled Jack.

The familiar voice in a room as alien as any in which he had ever stood got his attention. He turned and saw Jack on his knees next to Sean, gasping and choking on the floor. Patrick shuddered and threw the gun from him as if proximity to it mattered. He knelt beside Jack.

"Here, Patty. Put your hand here," said Jack. He pulled Patrick's hand toward Sean and placed it on the wound on his chest.

"Put some pressure on there," said Jack. "Like you mean it, Patty!"

He pushed down on Patrick's hand and Patrick felt his hand slide partially inside the wound. It was warm and the blood pulsated against him. He leaned his body weight onto the wound. He looked at Jack's hands, which were pressed against Sean's neck. Blood seeped through the fingers.

"You're okay, son," said Jack, his face only inches from Sean's. "You're okay. Hang in there. Stay with us."

"What about her? What should we . . . should we do something? Is there anything to do about her?" asked Patrick.

Jack glanced up and past Patrick.

"Not much we can do for her. Let's get this bleeding stopped."

Patrick increased the pressure on the chest wound. He wasn't sure what he was doing or how hard he should be pressing so he leaned on his hand as hard as he could without breaking Sean's ribs. He found that if he pushed hard enough with two of his fingers inside the wound, the pulsations felt less wet, so he stuck with the technique. He grew so fixated on his task that he dissociated the blood and the wound from the person and it wasn't until he looked up at the face that he remembered it was Sean under his hands.

Sean's face was gray beneath streaks of red. His mouth opened and closed like a goldfish, but only a thick spluttering sound came out. Patrick was surprised to see that his eyes were frantic but alert and he seemed to be trying to communicate something. He realized that the spluttering sound was forming the first syllable of his name. He leaned closer. Sean gasped something inaudible. He tried again but no words came out. Patrick leaned closer until his face was close to Sean's mouth. Sean made another gasping effort and spattered Patrick's cheek with blood, but again words failed to form.

"That's okay, Sean. That's okay," said Patrick.

Sean raised a weak arm. He put a clammy hand on Patrick's cheek and held it there. His hand trembled, and when he could no longer hold it upright, he let it fall on the back of Patrick's hand. An odd softness came over his face and he closed his eyes, but Patrick still felt a pulse on the fingers in the hole that their brother had made in his chest.

At some point, two men in uniform entered the room and Patrick could feel them around him but he did not see or did not take note of their faces. At some point, the room filled with numerous people in different uniforms, and gentle hands pulled him away from Sean and he let them. They put Sean on a gurney and wheeled him briskly from the room, then they did the same with Helen but not as briskly. People in suits asked Patrick questions and he marshaled all the focus he could, but it was like trying to tighten a spent muscle and he doubted the answers were of much use.

At some point he saw his own reflection in a mirror and did not recognize the wide-eyed hollow face that stared back. There was dried blood splattered on one cheek and smeared on the other, blood matted in his hair, and blood stains on his shirt. The stains were particularly dark and still very damp on one spot on his chest where he must have been rubbing his hand over and over again after they had taken Sean.

At some point, there were no more people in uniform and he and Jack were standing there alone. His face was wet and Jack's arm was around his shoulders. He could see Jack's fingers shaking in his periphery and he realized that it was not Jack's hand but his own shoulders that were making them shake.

CHAPTER NINETEEN

A few days after the first grass seedlings sprouted from the seeds sprinkled over the grave, after the electric crackle of fresh tragedy in the air had somewhat dissipated and the half-masted town had let the sharp edge of the shock wear down a bit, Patrick heard a knock on his door. He did not answer it. Well-wishers and reporters had long since worn out their welcome. The knocker, however, was insistent. Eventually, he gave in. He opened the door and, squinting into the light, saw Suzanne looking placidly up at him.

"Is he dead?" he asked.

"Oh, no, no," she said. "Nothing like that. Not to worry. I just came to see how you were."

"Ah," said Patrick. He was aware of his unshaven face and disheveled clothes and he wiped at the corners of his mouth as discreetly as possible.

"I spoke to Jack Kent. He mentioned that he hadn't seen you. I didn't see you at Helen's funeral either so I thought I'd come and check in on you."

"You went to Helen's funeral?" Patrick asked.

"Of course I did."

"I don't mean this to sound rude, but you went to your husband's mistress's funeral?"

"She was family," said Suzanne. "Just because she led an imperfect life doesn't mean I can't pay my respects. Are you going to invite me in?"

"Sure. Sorry," said Patrick.

He held the door open for Suzanne and turned on a light behind her.

"It's a bit of a mess," said Patrick.

"That's quite all right," said Suzanne. She cleared some papers and several empty bottles from a chair in the living room and took a seat.

"How is he?" asked Patrick.

"Improving, I think. He still can't speak. We don't know whether he'll ever fully regain speech. He has a little more movement on that right side and the doctors think he might be able to start rehab soon. So, we're optimistic. But you know how these things go. It's day-to-day."

Patrick looked at her sheepishly. "I'll try to make it over there to see him. I've been meaning to," he said.

"That's all right, Patrick. You'll come when you're ready."

Suzanne caught the distance in his eyes and cleared her throat. She folded her hands neatly on her lap. "I've come here today to ask something from you," she said.

"Of course. Anything."

"The truth of the matter is, even if he pulls through, he'll have neither the physical nor mental capacity to run the company." Her brow creased and she pressed a hand to her mouth. She took a deep breath and continued. "I'd like you to decide what we should do with it."

"Suzanne, if Sean could speak for himself, I think he'd tell you that he hates that idea. He and I never really . . . we don't see eye-to-eye on much."

"None of that matters now. I never could figure out why he held such resentment toward you. He would never give me a good reason. I suspect he was jealous. I think some part of him wished that he could have struck out on his own, maybe become more his own man. I think he envied your choices."

Patrick smiled. "So now you're asking me to give that up and join the company?"

"Nothing of the sort. I'm asking you to decide who should take over. You needn't run it yourself, but I think your father has earned the right to have one of his children decide what happens to his life's work. And no one who has ever spoken to me about you, good or bad, has ever said that you were unfair."

Patrick rubbed the back of his neck.

"And you have the authority here?"

"I have power of attorney for Sean, yes. Even if he regains full capability and is cleared to make decisions, he will agree with the choice I make in this matter."

"I have to ask you something. If it's too personal, you don't have to answer, but I have to ask," said Patrick.

"You're wondering if I knew that he was unfaithful," said Suzanne. "On some level, I'm sure I did. He had been different lately. I thought maybe it had something to do with everything that was happening with your father. It only seems clear after the fact."

"Why do you stay with him?"

"I'm married to him," she said.

"But if he didn't live up to his marital vows, why should you? Heartless as it sounds, it doesn't seem like you owe him anything."

"There has to be more to life than vengeance, Patrick. It seems that everyone today thinks they deserve a life that is simple and uncomplicated and without difficult choices. Well, you have to draw a line somewhere and put yourself on one side or the other. You have to choose something to believe in. I choose family."

"But how much is enough? At what point do you decide you've done the best you can and it's time to move on?"

"I suppose everyone decides that for themselves. But you don't 'move on' from your family. Even if you leave." She read Patrick's doubt and continued. "There's more to this than just he and I, Patrick. My children need me. And, right now, my husband's family needs me.

We need stability. My children need me to be strong. I want to do the right thing and, at the moment, that means asking you to do the right thing for your family."

Patrick shook his head slowly.

"I don't know. I don't know if I can do anything right now."

Suzanne patted the back of his hand.

"You've certainly been through a lot. That's understandable," she said, but it was not a retreat.

Patrick shrugged. "I don't even know where to start."

"Just think about it," she said. "Start with that. I have faith in you, Patrick."

Patrick looked at her, saw the warmth in her eyes that had always been there and a stiffness along her jaw that had not. He nodded.

"Good! Then it's settled. Let me know who you pick and we'll go from there." She stood to leave. "And Patrick, make sure you get outside at least once a day. Go for a walk. Go for a drive. Come and see the kids. Or just sit on the porch, if that's the best you can do. But get outside at least once a day. It'll be good for you."

It took three days for Patrick to go. He spent much of the first two sitting on his dock, trying to make himself move. At the end of the second day, he made it behind the wheel. On the third day, he made it out of his driveway. Once on the road, the act of driving took over and he kept going until he pulled into Jack's driveway.

It had been a beautiful plan. They sat in Jack's living room and Patrick held a glass of ice water that he did not drink while he listened to Jack explain it. With Jack and Doug conspiring together, no detail had been left out.

The plan they had decided on was not to resolve the matter in court. They had decided that a legal process would be too long, involved, and unpredictable. The more expedient method was to use Sean against himself. They would trigger his paranoia and his rage, exploit his ineptitude, and threaten to expose everything from falsified quarterly revenue reports to the very real affair he was having with Helen.

Once Sean was completely unhinged, once he was inches from the breaking point, they would offer him an out—a buyout of Sean's share of the company, in Henry's name but orchestrated by the conspirators. It would be an escape for Sean, a retreat to the more comfortable grounds of money without responsibility. By the time they made the offer, Sean would be so desperate that it would sound like they were doing him a favor.

"What happened? How did this thing go so wrong?" asked Patrick when Jack finished.

Jack hesitated. "A glitch," he said.

"What kind of 'glitch' got two people shot to hell?"

Again, Jack hesitated.

"It was an uncontrollable variable," he said, choosing his words carefully. "It's certainly of no consequence now."

"It was me, wasn't it?" asked Patrick.

"Patrick, this is not your fault."

He knew Jack would never admit it but it didn't matter. He knew that if at any point he had been more invested in any part of the events that had transpired since that night in Raleigh, or for that matter long before that night, it all might have been avoided. Jack's plan was, in its entirety, a backup plan, a hedge against Patrick's inaction. It had never occurred to Patrick that inaction could be an act of aggression or that inertia could put a series of events into motion.

"You told Bryan about Sean and Helen, didn't you?" said Patrick.

"I did," said Jack. "But please understand that what happened was not the desired outcome. We intended to put pressure on Sean, maybe push Bryan into playing more of a role. We didn't have anyone else . . . We didn't have any other means. It backfired terribly."

"You're telling me that you told a guy that his brother was sleeping with his wife, and you didn't consider violence a possibility?"

"We considered it. But given who we were talking about, we thought it was a low-risk probability. We were wrong."

"That's it? 'We were wrong'? Is that all it was to you? A 'low-risk probability' that didn't work out?"

"Patrick, I know you're angry with me. I can't presume to understand how you must feel. But I'm not going to lie to you. I did what I have always done—I made the best decision I could with the best information I had in the best interests of your father and the company. And this time, I failed. The outcome was tragic, and for that, I am truly sorry."

Patrick set his drink on a nearby table and leaned back on the couch. "I don't know. Bryan, Sean, Helen, myself. I'm mad at so many people I'm not sure there's room for you too, Jack. You're the only one who was trying to do something worth a damn."

"Patty, there's no reason to be angry at yourself. Your brother is alive solely because of your actions."

"He came in right behind me, Jack! How the hell did I not hear him? And then I stood there and watched while the gun went off. If I'd have moved faster, I might have been able to save her. Then Sean gets shot twice with me just frozen there. He's alive, sure. But not by much." He rubbed his forehead. He could feel his weeks-old headache creeping between his eyes. "You know what really bothers me? You know what thought I can't shake?"

"What's that?"

"Did you see his hand kind of twitch right before I grabbed him?"

"It happened so fast."

"I can't figure out whether or not I was next. I'm sure he was going to kill himself. I just wonder if maybe . . . I wonder if he lumped me in with them."

Jack cocked his head to one side and looked at Patrick, then looked away.

"Anyway, I guess that's not a question anyone can answer," said Patrick. "I doubt if even Bryan knows what he was going to do. And if he does, he won't tell me now."

A long quiet settled into the room. Patrick felt an intense sense of distance and separation he had never known in the town of his birth. He felt he should say something; lately, nothing good happened in his brain during long silences. Jack sat patiently.

"You know, you and your father are the only two people I know who truly love what they do," he said.

"You didn't love your work?" asked Patrick.

"I was good at it. I liked what I did and I felt it was important. But no, I never loved it. Your love of what you do, the sheer tenacity with which you hold onto it, is the part of your father I see most in you."

Patrick shrugged. "Yeah, well, a lot of good that's done me," he said. "Is he here?"

"Upstairs. Go ahead up."

"Is he . . . how is he today?"

"Not too bad. It's still early."

"Does he know what Bryan did?"

"I've told him everything. But it comes and goes."

Patrick went upstairs and knocked on the only closed door in the hall. Nobody answered so he let himself into a clean, white room with a neatly made bed. An open door led out to a small rooftop deck. Patrick saw his father seated in a deck chair reading a newspaper.

"Hey, Dad," said Patrick. "Can I join you?"

Henry eyed him warily, then jerked his head toward the only other chair on the deck. He snapped the paper to another page and continued reading. Patrick took a seat.

"You've heard about your fool brother, no doubt," said Henry without looking at him.

Patrick wasn't sure whether his father knew which of his sons he was addressing. He was uncertain whether or not he was the fool in question.

"What about him?"

"Went off the deep end and shot up the place," said Henry.

"I know. I was there, Dad."

"Of course you were. Of course you were," he muttered. "Suppose it's good then that no one got hurt worse than they did."

"Helen was killed. Hard to get hurt worse than that."

"Helen," he said, rolling his eyes from the paper to Patrick, "was a whore. We're better off without her."

"She was horrible," agreed Patrick. "But she didn't deserve what happened to her."

"We all get what we deserve," said Henry.

"You have Alzheimer's. You know that, right? Do you understand that?"

"We *all* get what we deserve," said Henry.

Patrick looked out at the waterway beyond Jack's backyard. From the height of the deck, he could see the distant outlines of the houses on the island. He wondered if his father saw what he saw when he looked out at the water and the land that they both knew so well. He wondered if it felt like home to his father, if he drew from the water the same sense of stability and self. Or if he saw only money and power, an array of things from which to extract other things.

"I need to talk to you about who should take over," said Patrick.

Henry looked at him suspiciously. He folded the newspaper and slapped it onto the table.

"And why would you think you have any say in that?" he asked.

"You've got a son in jail and another in the hospital who's not likely to fully recover. You're running out of people to trust."

"I'll run the company. I got it this far, didn't I? Jack and I can manage."

"Did you ever consider putting Jack in charge?" asked Patrick.

"No, I didn't," said Henry firmly.

"Come on, Dad. You honestly thought Sean and Bryan were more capable than him?"

"You think you're so smart? Jack *asked* me not to consider him. Years ago. He doesn't want to be in charge."

"I don't believe that," said Patrick.

"When he's done, when he's ready to retire, he wants to be able to walk away from this job clean and you just can't do that when you're in charge. It eats up all your thoughts. Jack wants to be able to step away and spend time with his family without his work hanging over him. That's the problem."

"Jack's problem is that he cares about his family?"

"Son, if you're going to find someone to run a company, if you're looking for true greatness in a leader, you've got to find someone so dedicated and so loyal that the job is their obsession. It has to consume him so much that it damn near kills off the rest of him. It has to be their entire world, and if the other things in their life get squeezed out or pushed aside, then so be it. The job *is* their family."

"And you think Sean and Bryan fit that—"

"Sean and Bryan are family, in the more conventional sense," said Henry, "and I chose them because of that. God knows I didn't think they'd screw it up as badly as they did. And you, well, you weren't interested at all. Your heart's not in it."

"Come on, Dad. Don't start with me again."

"I'm not starting anything. I'm saying there weren't any other good options. As for you, I guess sometimes a man just has to choose his own way and that's what you did. I guess that's what I did years ago, too. And maybe that's not all bad."

Patrick looked sidelong at Henry. It was the most understanding thing his father had ever said to him and he had to look to see if there was a catch, but Henry said nothing more. Patrick looked back out toward the water because he did not want his father to see his eyes.

"Now, on your way out, send someone up to clean up these dishes," said Henry. "If Marie comes home and the house is like this, she's going to be very irritated."

Patrick looked at his father and saw a blankness where his whole life he had only seen sharp-eyed imperiousness. He tried to see if there was some trace of awareness of what he had said, some isolated lonely last-ditch outpost still standing vigilant over all the images the primordial eyes had gathered over the course of their weather-worn life. There was nothing, and the fact that he had not expected to find anything did not lessen Patrick's sadness.

Patrick found Jack downstairs.

"It has to be you," said Patrick.

Jack's stare pierced him. "Are you the one who has to make the choice?"

"I am. Suzanne came to see me."

"Ah," said Jack. He took a deep breath and exhaled slowly. "I can certainly understand the logic there. But it can't be me. I can't go from who I am to who your father is."

"I need you to do it," said Patrick. "Just long enough to train someone else. If you don't, the whole thing collapses in on itself and you know it. So I want you to take over my father's company and I want you to run it until you feel confident that Doug Castin can take over for you."

"Doug Castin?"

"You seem surprised."

"He's shown nothing but promise and his loyalty is beyond question. He's just so young."

"Exactly. I want you to mold him as you see fit. I barely know the kid, but everything about him tells me that he'd absolutely become that job."

Jack rubbed his jaw with the back of his hand. "Of course you know what this choice means, as far as your family is concerned?"

"It means that there won't be an O'Reilly running Coastal Seafood. But it also means that Coastal Seafood will survive."

"Your father fought for years to keep the company privately owned. He wanted it to stay in the family. You're sure you're comfortable going against that arrangement?"

"It was never a family business, Jack. That's what my father never understood. It destroyed my family. It's strange as hell to say, but I don't think the O'Reilly family can coexist with its own company."

"I think you're probably right," said Jack. He reached out his hand and Patrick shook it. For an instant, Jack's hard-set eyes revealed the ancient sadness of long-carried fatigue. Then he blinked and it was gone. He gave Patrick half a smile. "But it's a goddamn shame, isn't it?"

CHAPTER TWENTY

He felt the heat on the back of his neck even though it was an uncharacteristically gray day for midsummer. As he worked his way through the pile of cut wood, hammer hit nail in a steady, driving rhythm. The rain had stayed away but the sky had not cleared and the marsh was hot and felt sluggish, as if neither tides nor living things had planned to do anything that day but wait for the rain that would not come.

He had plenty of work; he was at least grateful for that. He was always busiest after a hurricane and he had gotten backed up after what had happened. It might even have been too much work, which was even better. Perhaps he would have to push himself harder and leave himself with no energy at the end of the day to think about anything for a few weeks, maybe even a month. He wasn't sure what might be different or better in a month other than that it would be a month later, but it was something.

Mr. Macready was understanding about the delay. He told Patrick to come back when he got his feet under him, that there was no need to rush. He said there were "circumstances beyond his control," and Patrick had wished that were true but did not say so. When he did make it back to finish his work, Mr. Macready left him alone and Patrick appreciated that. He was sure that he, like the rest of the town, had seen the reports that had dominated the local news and seeped into the national media. He must have had questions, and Patrick appreciated that he did not ask them.

He would be done soon and there was still plenty of daylight so he did not rush and the finished part of the dock inched ever farther out over the water. He knew it made no difference, but he thought he might feel better once he had completed the job that he had been working on when things had gone so badly awry and people had gotten smashed up and shot apart and he had done nothing to stop any of it.

It had all settled out finally. He was pleased about that. The story was the story for a while, then the backstory as people occupied themselves with somber-voiced speculations, of varying degrees of accuracy, concerning the secret sinister underbelly of the O'Reilly family. Finally, however, the demand for information and the supply of answers reached stasis, the story dried up, and the reporters and the inquisitors left town. So if the pain was still left, if the town was still sore and uncertain and dismayed by the things that had happened, at least the shock and the out-of-towners had dissipated.

The matters of business about which Patrick cared so little had also been carried out effectively and, from Patrick's grateful perspective, opaquely. There was still legal wrangling to be done but, for the most part, the transfer of ownership had been handled expertly by Jack and Doug and whoever else they trusted.

The business of the company was far less interesting than Bryan's moment of violence, so the mundane and important details of the transfer had been handled with almost no attention from the town that had so much at stake in the company's future. Bryan had inadvertently created a spectacular diversion, had drawn the town's eye away from the unsettling instability in the ownership of the company that the town relied on until that instability had been rectified. Discharging a handgun into his wife and brother was thus the best business move Bryan had ever made for the long-term well-being of Coastal Seafood.

With matters of both the town and the company situated at some point outside of Patrick's periphery, all matters fell away from him except for time and work, the former over which he wielded no influence and the latter over which he exercised near-complete dominion. Despite the irreconcilable gap between the helplessness of one and the control of the other, the two ideas were inextricably intertwined around Patrick. Time pressed on him from the outside and the work pushed out from inside him and the two forces created an equilibrium that was the only thing that kept Patrick upright and moving through the world.

Time and work were the last undestroyed temples, and he worshipped at them without reservation.

The hammer fell for the last time. He reflexively wiped his hand over the indentation to make sure the nail head did not stick out. He ran his hand along the final board to make sure it was flush to the end of the dock and at all points equidistant from the preceding board. Then he stood on stiff knees and, one eye squinting, stared down the line of the dock from marsh to house, first on one side of the dock and then on the other. Finally, he walked slowly down the length of the dock, tugging on the railings to make sure they weren't too loose and checking all the planks to ensure no nails had been missed. Satisfied, he gathered his tools and wiped his hands on his pants.

He leaned his forearms on the railing and looked out at the water. It was the same marsh, the same waterway, and the same island in the distance, the same sky and sun, the same salt and air that he had always known despite the thousands of changes that had come in great titanic blasts and tiny imperceptible shifts over the miniscule span of time that his life had comprised.

He remembered a time during his youth when he had been deeply saddened by the awareness that the water had been there for so long and would outlast him by so great a scale that no matter how much time he spent on the water or how much of it he breathed in or how much it meant to him, he would see but a tiny, insignificant speck of the life of the marsh.

But as he stood there staring out at the flat calm of the slack tide, he drew comfort from the awesome power of the great, yawning chasm of time. His life would be a sliver of a reflection of a moment on the water. His work would rot and fall away, would sink into the ground and be absorbed into the water, and he could think of no better end for his life's toil. So would time absorb all else in its slow and certain path, all of his memories and reflections, his choices and his mistakes, his ability to feel guilt and the recollection of warm, pulsing blood pushing against his hands. He felt absolved, in a sense, that there was no decision he or anyone else could have made, or failed to make, that would matter at all once enough time had passed. Time outlasts sins. People do not.

And though it saddened him to at last ask something more of the water and air and land that had always been enough for him, he leaned over the rail and, seeing his reflection, asked that the water be so vast and time so immense as to allow him to slip unnoticed amongst them and live the rest of his days in peace.

ACKNOWLEDGEMENTS

I am grateful for all who were positive, with special thanks to the following:

Jenni and the kids, of whom I ask too much.

My friends, old and new, upon whom I've leaned so heavily for so long, with particular attention to Jeremy Hilburn and Tony Baker, who were always what I needed them to be; to Tony Muscio, who has believed in me since five minutes after we met and has been impatient for this book in all the best ways; and to Matt Lisi, who has, from time to time, been the last thread holding me to sanity.

My long-suffering parents who, I swear, were not subjects in this story; my brothers Tim and Mike and their families; and my extended family, most of whom were supportive, none more vociferously than Aunt Dot (who has always wanted to be a writer).

Everyone I've worked alongside at jobs that don't come with acknowledgement pages.

Everyone I knew who died but refused to leave me.

The faculty, staff, and students in NC, especially Clyde, David, Bekki, Nina, and Robert.

Bruce Bortz, Katie Mead-Brewer, Jen Herchenroeder, Shani Sladowsky, and everyone at Bancroft Press who worked so hard to make this happen.

And finally, William Shakespeare, who came up with all the good stories so the rest of us don't have to.

ABOUT THE AUTHOR

Photo Courtesy of Carson Vaughan

Drew Krepp was born on the North Fork of Long Island and grew up in Fayetteville, North Carolina. He graduated from Cornell University with a B.A. in English and a concentration in 19th century American literature before studying creative writing at the University of North Carolina Wilmington.

In the intervening years, he has worked as a lawn and garden center helper, a kennel worker, a bartender, a dishwasher in a sorority house, a pizza delivery driver, a mailroom clerk at a law school, a customer account rep at a sign shop, an organ-transplant courier, a production assistant for a non-profit arts organization, a boat maintenance/repair tech, a carpenter/handyman, a reader for a literary journal, and a graduate teaching assistant.

In addition to Fayetteville and Long Island, he has lived in Raleigh, North Carolina; Hampstead, North Carolina; Ithaca, New York;

Providence, Rhode Island; Philadelphia, Pennsylvania; Washington, DC; and on a sailboat in the Northwest Harbor of the Patapsco River before settling in the Hampden neighborhood of North Baltimore. He now divides his time between Wilmington and Baltimore, where he lives with his wife Jenni, their two children, and the world's least aggressive cat in a venerable brick rowhouse that leaks more than the above mentioned sailboat did.

His story, "The Brackish," was selected by Women's Prize for Fiction winner and bestselling author AM Homes for inclusion in *The Masters Review*, which annually publishes a ten-story collection showcasing the best in graduate-level writing from students in MA, MFA, and PhD creative writing programs. The aim in producing this collection is to expose progressive, diverse, and well-crafted writing to agents, editors, and readers.

The Salt Marsh King is his first published novel.